BOOKER & FITCH

CW01510979

DEATH
on the
Towpath

LIZ HEDGECOCK   PAULA HARMON

WHITE
RHINO
BOOKS

ISBN-13: 979-8870062242

*To our English teachers,
who loved the subject and put up with us...*

CHAPTER 1

'I can't believe how many romance novels have gone,' said Zach, slumping in the chair on the deck of the Book Barge. 'Reckon it's the weather?'

Fi refilled her assistant's glass of iced water and grinned. 'Reckon it's the venue.' She waved the jug at Spetisham Hall, which stood in neo-classical splendour, looking down on its luxurious gardens and a long stretch of the River Wyvern, as it had for two hundred years. 'They were mostly Regency romances and there's a Regency theme throughout the fete. When we were asked to bring the Book Barge, I thought it might be worth stocking up.'

Zach nodded. 'Good call.' He'd started working for her after the murder at Hazeby Little Theatre the previous year, keen on proving himself and learning everything he could about business.

Under a cloudless blue sky, the gardens and

riverbank were filled with multicoloured stalls and marquees swarming with hordes of people. Perhaps the Burlingtons, who'd had the house built, were spinning in their graves, but their descendants were realists and wanted to maximise the estate's potential. Day-trippers visited the grounds and parts of the house all year round, it was a wedding venue, and on May Bank Holiday weekend, they hosted a three-day fete. This year the events manager, Simon Davison, had asked Fi to bring the Book Barge and moor near the Burlingtons' boathouse. In the meadow, he'd given Jade Fitch space for a Crystal Dreams stall. The weather had been glorious, allowing Fi to open an extra sales area on the deck which Nerys was running. Business had been brisk.

Zach drained his glass. 'Here come more customers. I'll manage. You go for a break.'

'I won't be long. I'll see if I can find Dylan – Stan will have had enough of a walk by now.'

Zach grinned. 'Say hello to the inspector for me.'

Fi ignored him.

It was hot by the river, and even hotter among the tents. The Crystal Dreams stall was only recognisable by the sign on its gazebo and a glimpse of the pink streaks in Jade's curls. It was a metre deep in customers. There was no point in making things worse by trying to say hello.

The food area was buzzing, and despite the

sweltering heat, the hot-food vendors had long queues.

But a metre or so away, the community policing tent was empty except for Inspector Marcus Falconer and a young constable. Both were peering at a laptop. Fi smoothed her summer dress and puffed her hair a little, then entered.

Marcus smiled and came over. 'Can I help you, madam? Would you like to try this computer quiz on home security?'

'Not really. I fancy a walk.'

Marcus looked at the constable. 'Would you mind if I leave you for a few minutes?'

The constable shrugged. 'Reckon I can beat off the rush, sir. When you're back, can I get food? The smell's driving me barmy.'

'It's a deal.'

Fi and Marcus stepped out of the tent. 'How's business?' he asked, kissing her then taking her hand.

'Fantastic. I can't be out too long, but I thought I'd say hello. It's been a mad few days and it feels like ages since that pub lunch on Thursday.'

'I've missed you. Let's go out again soon.'

Fi pulled a face. 'Maybe after the exams. Dylan's having a bit of a crisis about his GCSEs.'

'You haven't got him locked up revising, have you?'

'Not today. They don't start for two weeks, so he can have the weekend off now.'

'Very generous.'

Fi smiled, but she sensed his tension. 'How about Leo's revision for his AS levels?'

Marcus grunted. 'Our tent's getting more footfall than his course notes. I hope Dylan's not looking to him for tips.'

'I don't imagine they discuss swotting. They're following different paths, anyway.'

Since Marcus and Fi had been going out on a fairly regular basis, their sons had become acquainted, though all they had in common was gaming. Dylan already knew of Leo through school, but Leo hadn't known Dylan. Fi remembered that when she'd been at school, younger students often knew the older students, while the older students thought the younger ones unworthy of their interest. She also recalled that only the 'interesting' older students were well known: class clowns, flirts, boundary pushers. Not the serious, heads-down types, like Fi. Which type was Leo?

'I wish I knew what path Leo was following,' said Marcus. 'He won't tell his mother or me. Just grunts and tells us to mind our own business.'

'He's always polite to me.'

Marcus squeezed her hand. 'He likes you. I daresay it's no fun being a copper's son and his stepdad rubs that in a bit, but I hope he's not doing anything stupid. If Dylan ever tells you anything you think I should know…'

'I doubt he will, but if I get any hint, I'll tell you.'

They wound their way through the stalls and entered the dark interior of the music tent, which was having an open mic hour while it prepare to announce which amateur bands would perform at a one-day music festival in the streets of Hazeby in two weekends' time.

Dylan was sitting on the grass with his friends and Stan the dog. Max and Alfie were comparing something on their phones. Stan was snoozing. But Dylan was staring at a girl who was pouring every ounce of a sixteen-year-old's angst into 'I Will Survive'. There was no mistaking his adoration. It disappeared the second Stan spotted Fi, made his peculiar woof and pulled at his lead.

Dylan stumbled to his feet and came over. 'Hi, Marcus. Can you take Stan, Mum?'

'Of course. I thought Chloe was helping her mum on a craft stall.'

Dylan went crimson. 'She's allowed time off, isn't she?'

'Of course. I meant, er… Feel free to bring any friends round to the barge when we're closed to the public. Including Chloe, if her mum doesn't need her to help pack up.'

Dylan's face went darker. 'Yeah, yeah. Don't go on.'

Alfie and Max were watching them and Chloe's song was nearing its defiant end. It seemed cruel to stay, so Fi nudged Marcus and they made their way outside.

Before she could say anything, Marcus extracted his mobile. 'Yes? Oh. I won't be long. Bye.' He turned to Fi. 'All of a sudden, there's an influx of people demanding information about Wyvernshire policing from someone senior. I'm not sure if they're troublemakers or from the Women's Institute. From past experience, that could be one and the same. I'd best go. See you on Wednesday?'

'Sounds great.' They shared a kiss and Fi returned to the boat with Stan to give Zach a break.

Most of the customers were on the deck, where Nerys seemed to be managing well enough. Fi put Stan in the private area of the boat and settled down to sell books.

'Isn't it lovely?'

Fi saw Simon the events manager descend into the boat behind a woman in her early thirties. He led her across the shop floor with a smile broader than his usual cool, professional one. 'Bianca, this is Fi Booker, owner of this wonderful shop. Fi, this is Bianca Spencer. She went to uni with me a million years ago.'

'Less of the millions, Simon,' said Bianca, shaking Fi's hand. 'You're making me feel ancient.' She was curvy and pretty, with thick curly brown hair, tanned skin and dark-blue eyes.

He blushed. 'Oh. Sorry. I didn't mean…'

'Don't be daft, Simon,' said Bianca. 'You never did know when I was teasing you! It does seem like a million years ago. I remember coming to Hazeby and Spetisham with you a couple of times. I barely recognise it now. A book barge and a crystal shop! And an arts festival, and the music festival in a fortnight. It's great.' She looked around the inside of the shop. Shafts of light were slanting through the windows. 'This is magical. If something like this had existed when I was a student, you'd never have got me out. Mind if I explore, even if I don't buy? There's never much space in hand luggage.'

'Of course.' Fi watched Bianca stride towards the shelves, then glanced at Simon. He was following her every move as she made her way to the travel section and touched the books with gentle reverence. She selected a slim Edwardian volume about Spain and perused it with her head on one side.

He shook himself a little and turned back to Fi. 'Old friend, you know. *Good* friend.' Again, that slight flush. 'She went travelling after uni and never returned. Her parents had split up and she didn't like her stepdad, from what I remember. But even if that hadn't been the case, I think she'd have gone anyway. Not like boring old unimaginative me, barely moving

7

twenty miles from the university.'

'You're not unimaginative,' said Fi. 'You've made the hall a great local attraction without cheapening it. I really appreciate you inviting me to join the fete this year.'

'The Book Barge is a great attraction,' said Simon. 'I should have thought of it before. That's why I'm here: to say thanks, and also... If we do a Christmas Fayre and we can work out a safe way to get people to the riverbank, would you be up for it?'

'Definitely.'

'Wonderful. It's still an idea, but I think it has legs.'

'I'm sure it has.' Fi's mind began to whirr with ideas and images.

'It's been a great weekend. Reconnecting with an old friend has made it even better.' Simon's gaze settled on Bianca, who was returning with the book.

'This looks great,' she said, 'and not so heavy the airline will notice. Not that it'll matter for a while.'

'Oh,' said Simon, very casually. 'Thinking of staying?'

'For a while.' Bianca handed Fi the book, her smile faltering a little as Simon beamed.

They left just before Dylan came down the steps alone.

'Are you all right?' said Fi, before she could stop herself. 'I wasn't expecting you for ages.'

'Aren't I allowed? Am I getting in the way of you and Marcus?'

'Of course not.' Fi stared at him. Dylan had never expressed anything negative about Marcus before. 'I suppose Chloe's helping her mum pack up.'

'What? Yeah, I guess.'

'Max and Alfie?'

'Heading home on the shuttle bus, I think. I'm going to my cabin. Er . . . revision.'

'It's still the bank holiday, Dylan,' said Fi. 'Give yourself a break.'

He said nothing, his face solemn and anxious. It was an unfamiliar expression that chilled her.

'There's no reason you should fail,' she said. 'And exam results don't define you as a person. They're a snapshot of a few weeks in a long life. There's always a different path if things don't work out the way you planned. You'll be fine.'

He didn't answer at first, then shrugged. 'I'm still going to my cabin.' He gave her a lopsided smile. 'Is there anything to eat?'

'That's more like it,' said Fi. 'I'll make you a snack at six. Is that OK? Do you still want Jade to take you back to Hazeby this evening, so you can stay at Max's?'

'Yeah.' He ruffled her hair and gave her the briefest hug.

After a few moments, his music drifted into the

9

shop. He must have the volume of his headphones up to the max. Fi would never have been able to study with music that loud, but maybe Dylan was wired differently. Or maybe it was something else. She remembered his face as he'd looked at Chloe and was reminded of Simon's as he'd looked at Bianca – the 'good friend' he'd had at university maybe fifteen years ago.

Fi grinned. There was nothing like first love. At least she and Marcus weren't that bad.

Hopefully.

CHAPTER 2

In her head, Jade counted to ten. 'I'm very sorry, but I've run out of the small cauldrons. I have a couple of medium ones left, if they're any good.'

'I've been waiting patiently, on a hot day, and now I find out you don't even have what I came for.' The speaker was a youngish, plumpish woman, whose fringe was plastered to her forehead with sweat. Her T-shirt said *Don't Worry, Be Happy*.

'As I said, I'm sorry. It's the last day of a three-day festival, and it's been busy.' Jade waved a hand at her depleted stall. 'What you see is all I have left. If you'd like to choose something different...'

'I'll take a medium,' snapped the woman.

'Excellent. Would you like a bag?'

The woman shook her head. 'Will you do it for the price of a small one, seeing as that's what I wanted?'

Jade raised her eyebrows. 'I'll take a pound off.'

'I suppose that'll have to do.' She fished a card out of her jeans pocket and touched it to the card reader. 'Hopefully you've learnt for next time. If there is one.' She picked up the cauldron and ambled away, swinging it by the handle. Behind her, Jade mimed wiping the sweat from her brow.

A cheerful woman in a floral maxi dress stepped up. 'She was a ray of sunshine, wasn't she? Maybe she'll mix a happiness potion in that cauldron of hers. You should've sold her a large one!'

Jade forced herself to smile. It had been a long day. No, a long weekend. And it had had none of the usual qualities of a normal long weekend: namely, sleeping in, brunch, slobbing on the sofa, maybe a walk, and a few glasses of wine with a friend. Instead, she had been standing at a trestle table in the sun for three days, feeling like a butterfly on a pin.

Then again, that had partly been her own fault. When Fi had mentioned the festival at Spetisham Hall, Jade had imagined a relaxed affair where she and Fi would share a stall, cover for each other, nip off for cheese rolls and cups of tea, then head to a convenient pub in the evening. It had come as a shock to find out that Fi was bringing *Coralie*.

'So you'll be on the boat?'

'Well, yes. Spetisham's by the river. Where did you think you'd sleep?'

Jade grinned. 'I thought I might get lucky.'

Fi rolled her eyes. 'In the event that you don't, there's the sofabed.'

Jade had attempted to press-gang her son Hugo into helping. Again, that hadn't gone entirely as planned.

'Of course, Mummy!' he had exclaimed. 'I'd love to spend time in Hazeby and help you out.'

'Not Hazeby, Hugo,' Jade said, as patiently as she knew how. Honestly, for an intelligent lad, Hugo could be remarkably dim at times. 'At the festival, in Spetisham.'

'But you're always telling me that Netta doesn't cope well on her own in the shop for any length of time,' Hugo said, very reasonably. 'After all, Crystal Dreams is your main business. It would be terrible if something happened to threaten that while you weren't there. Anyway, didn't you say Fi's going? And your next-door neighbour, what's-his-name. You'll have oodles of helpers.'

'Maybe,' Jade conceded.

'Of course you will. Besides, if you're sleeping on Fi's boat, with Fi, Dylan and maybe Marcus too, there won't be room for me.'

Jade fumed, silently. 'All right. I'll change the bedlinen before I leave.'

'No need, Mummy. While we've been talking, I've found a smashing Airbnb in the town centre.'

'Sounds like you've got it all worked out,' Jade

said, with a hint of sourness.

As it turned out, Jade had not got it worked out at all. Fi had brought both Zach and Nerys to help her, and had interspersed her shifts on the Book Barge with walking Stan and ambling around the stalls chatting to people. Occasionally she visited Jade's stall, sometimes bringing a cold drink, which Jade was grateful for, but the press of people waiting to be served meant they had barely exchanged a word during working hours.

The festival had run into the evening, with dramatic performances and bands in a central marquee. Not wanting to lose business, Jade's stall had stayed open. The result was that when Jade finally did call time and drag her aching legs over *Coralie*'s gangplank, she generally ate a bowl of whatever was on offer, drank a glass of wine, then fell into a deep sleep on the sofabed. She felt a bit bad about being such an antisocial guest.

And as for Rick...

A few days before the festival, Jade had suggested they could drive down together in Rick's van. 'It would be nice to have company on the journey,' she said. 'Like a sort of road trip.'

Rick looked puzzled. 'Spetisham's no distance,' he said. 'Anyway, you'll have your stuff and I'll have my stuff. Plus band stuff.'

'Oh yes, band stuff. I forgot.' It had completely

slipped her mind that Rick had done a few gigs in Spetisham. 'We can still help each other, right? Cover each other's tables?'

'I'm pretty much sorted, thanks. Shelley's lending a hand. She fancies the festival anyway, and this way she gets a freebie.'

'Shelley? As in your ex, Shelley?'

'That's the one. She loves a good festival. Plus it'll help with her research.'

Mindful that she'd asked more than enough questions already, Jade confined herself to raising her eyebrows.

'She's doing a Masters in the persistence of ancient English customs.'

'Right,' said Jade.

To be fair, Rick had wandered over every so often and asked how she was doing. But every time she glanced at his stall, he and Shelley appeared to be sharing a joke. Shelley herself was fortyish, with a long brown plait, laughing blue eyes, and the sort of curvy figure that suited a smock top and a long tiered skirt. No wonder Rick was having a good time. Such a good time that he closed his stall at four every day and went off to enjoy the evening festivities. Jade felt as if there was a permanent black cloud above her head, threatening rain.

Next time there's a festival, I'll be prepared, she thought. *If there is a next time. I might stay in the shop and send Netta instead.*

And then there were Marcus and Fi. To give them credit, they weren't one of those couples who canoodled at every opportunity and made everyone sick. And going out with a copper certainly wasn't Jade's idea of a good time: far too much scope for knuckle rapping. But sometimes she caught a look in Fi's eyes when she was looking at Marcus, or talking about Marcus, or possibly just thinking about Marcus, and it made her want to say something childish and silly.

Not that I'm jealous, she thought. *Men are nothing but trouble. While Marcus is one of the better examples, Fi's welcome to him.*

So when Rick came over at five and asked if she'd like a hand packing up, Jade had a response ready.

'I'll manage, thanks.' She waved an airy hand at her two trestle tables, which had items dotted here and there. 'There isn't much left. About a box worth.'

'You've done well, then,' said Rick. 'I've shifted lots of small woodcarvings, but most of the expensive stuff – inlaid chests and whatnot – will be coming home with me. It's all packed now, though. So if you did want a hand…'

'As I said, I can manage.' Jade fished a packing crate from under the trestle table, took out pieces of bubble wrap and a roll of tape, and began to wrap her one remaining cauldron. 'Did Shelley have a good time?' she asked, concentrating on placing the tape just right.

'She did, yes. She took a video of the Morris dancers and managed to interview them afterwards. She reckons there's a piece to be written about adult men's motivation to join a dance troupe.'

'Motivation to make a fool of yourself in public,' said Jade, placing the cauldron in the crate and reaching for a small box of crystals. That could go in unwrapped.

'Maybe they enjoy it and don't care what people think,' said Rick.

'Up to them.' Jade made a parcel of books and put bubble wrap round them. The tape squealed as she pulled it.

'Yes,' said Rick.

'So, are you and Shelley heading off in a bit?'

'We will be. Hope Bertha behaves herself for you.'

'She will. She's been like a new car since George got under her bonnet.' This wasn't strictly true, as Bertha still had a tendency to cough and splutter when required to go uphill or travel at more than forty miles an hour. But she started first time, more often than not, and never took more than three attempts to get going.

'Right, I'll be off then.' Rick strolled away, turning once to wave.

Jade finished packing, lugged the box all the way

17

to the car park, cursing the heat, then went to *Coralie*. She had agreed to take Dylan home with her, as Fi was staying another night. She crossed the gangplank and knocked at the wheelhouse door. 'Anyone home?' she called.

Dylan opened the door. 'Mum's walking Stan,' he said. 'She said to say goodbye to you. I've got your bag here, inside the door. I only need a lift to Max's, anyway. His mum said I could stay over.'

Does no one want to spend any time with me? thought Jade. 'OK, let's go. I'm expecting traffic.' She strode to the field where Bertha was parked, Dylan trailing after her. Most people had gone already, but she recognised Rick's van, a blue Transit with *R Jennings, Furniture Restoration and Frames* on one side and *The Wayfarers – Stirring Folk Music* on the other. *What's he still doing here?*

'Come on, Dylan,' she said, slinging her bag on the back seat and getting in.

'Wow,' said Dylan. 'Can I wind down the window with the little handle?'

'Fill your boots. But buckle up first.' She avoided looking out of her side window towards Rick's van as she turned the key.

'*Ni-ni-ni-ni-ni-ni-ni-ni—*' said Bertha.

'Not now,' muttered Jade.

'Is that supposed to happen?' asked Dylan.

Jade suppressed a growl. 'Come on, Bertha.'

'*Ni-ni-ni-ni-nip-nip-nip-niii-aaaah*,' Bertha sighed.

Out of the corner of her eye, Jade saw the window of Rick's van descend. He put his elbow on the sill, but said nothing. She could see Shelley in the passenger seat beyond, also watching. 'Come *on*, Bertha,' she urged.

'Do we need to call the AA?'

'No, Dylan, we do not.' She took a deep breath and turned the key again.

'*Nip-nip-nip-brrRROOMM.*' Bertha let out an impressive roar. Rick gave her a thumbs-up sign and his window closed.

Jade moved off smoothly, willing Bertha not to play up, not to stall, and most importantly, not to give Rick any reason to pull up beside her and play the good Samaritan.

'Did you enjoy the festival, Jade?' asked Dylan.

'Yeah, it was fun,' she replied. But right now, all she wanted was to get Bertha safely home, put her pyjamas on, and veg out on the sofa with the sort of carb-laden dinner that no respectable rural festival would let through its doors. Everything else could wait.

CHAPTER 3

To Fi's disappointment, Jade and Dylan were gone when she returned from walking Stan.

But then, Jade must be even more shattered than Fi and desperate to get home. When Fi had been able to visit her stall it had been swamped, and every evening Jade came back to *Coralie* exhausted. And there was Fi with Zach all day and Nerys from eleven till four thirty.

Perhaps she should have offered one of them to help, though they were rushed off their feet too, but she'd assumed Hugo would turn up. Yet he hadn't come, even on Sunday.

At least Rick had said that morning, on a brief visit, that he'd help Jade pack up, which meant Fi hadn't had to worry about her while she and Zach did the same.

Sorry I missed you, she messaged to Jade. *Are you*

free tomorrow evening? I've got a bottle of sparkly with our name on it. We deserve a reward – you especially.

There was no reply, but doubtless once Jade had finished unloading and catching up with Hugo, she'd either go for a drink with Rick, as she sometimes did, or more likely crash in front of the TV.

Fi poured herself a glass of wine and watched people dismantle the last marquee. A group of litter-pickers collected the last bits of debris, their voices carrying but the words indecipherable. Then they were gone and the world fell silent but for the lapping of the river and evening birdsong. Spetisham Hall looked down on its gardens in peace again. Fi could almost imagine it breathing a sigh of relief.

It was odd, sitting on *Coralie*'s cleared deck and knowing she was all alone. Not unpleasant, but odd.

It was a shame Marcus was on duty until Wednesday, but it was nice to be on her own with her thoughts for a change. No one asking for books that didn't exist or that she hadn't got. No Nerys chattering. No Zach worrying if he'd made a mistake. No wondering how Dylan would respond to whatever she said – agreeing, laughing, mocking, sulking? Why did adolescence have to be so unpredictable and agonising for everyone involved?

Fi tousled Stan's head and noticed her glass was empty. She went down to the galley and returned a short while later with a Greek salad, flatbread drizzled in olive oil and another glass of wine. The sun was low in an apricot sky and the shadows were growing longer.

I wish you were here, she messaged to Marcus.

'Er, hello?'

Fi jumped, wine sloshing over the edge of her glass. On the bank end of the gangplank stood Bianca Spencer, wearing a lacy shrug with her sundress.

'I thought everyone had gone,' said Fi. 'I mean, I suppose Simon's still finishing up and, er, so on. Are you having a walk while you wait for him?'

'Oh. Um… I thought I'd come and chat with you. Is that OK?' Bianca was hugging herself and seemed anxious. Fi wondered if she had committed to spending time with Simon, regretted it, and wanted help to escape. Not that Fi could do much.

'Is everything all right?'

'Er… Sort of.'

'Come aboard. Would you like some wine?'

'Thanks, but I can't. My car's in the car park and I'm going to my hotel later. I won't take up too much time.'

'Something else?'

'No, thanks.' Bianca sat on the edge of the other deckchair, putting her small backpack in her lap.

Fi was nonplussed. If Bianca wasn't waiting for Simon, why had she stayed? Had the book she'd bought turned out to be more valuable than Fi had realised? But it had been sold fair and square and Fi wouldn't expect anything extra. Or… Bianca had said how much she loved the Book Barge. Perhaps she was thinking of starting a similar venture herself. 'Did you want to look round again? If you're staying in the area, I'm sailing back to Hazeby first thing tomorrow and I'll be open by nine-thirty.'

'It's not that. Please sit down, too. Is this your dog? He's lovely.' Bianca reached over to stroke Stan, who peered at her with his head on one side.

In the dusk Bianca was prettier than ever, her lashes long and dark, curls coiling around her cheeks. She sat up straight, reached into her bag and handed Fi two photographs. 'I want to show you these. Can you see them OK? Should I use the torch on my phone?'

In the first photograph, a man in his thirties sat at a small table with a cup of coffee in front of him. He was laughing.

More to the point, he was Fi's dead husband, Gavin.

It was how she remembered him. How he came to her in her dreams sometimes. That infectious laugh, those twinkling eyes. He'd looked like that the last time she'd seen him, fifteen years ago. Even if it had no longer been her who made him laugh or twinkle.

She felt her hands tremble, but said nothing. How

did Bianca have a photo of Gavin from around the time he'd died?

Fi glanced at the second photo, then stared. It looked like the same man, now in his forties. Fuller in the face, greying at the temples, laughter lines round his eyes. She flipped the photos back and forth then compared them, wishing it wasn't dusk. The faces weren't at the same angle. They weren't in the same light, but... She licked her lips and took a deep breath. 'What... Who am I looking at?'

'Your husband.'

'My husband's dead.'

'His body wasn't found, was it?'

'No, but the police said it must have been swept out to sea. The river he drove into was in flood. It was only by chance his . . . his girlfriend wasn't swept out too. If he'd survived, he'd have got in touch with his mother at the very least.'

Bianca shook her head. 'He owed money, didn't he?'

Fi didn't reply. The photographs were growing sticky in her hand.

'I know it's hard to believe,' said Bianca. 'I... I'm in shock too. The thing is— He's *my* husband. Or at least, I thought he was. And I thought he was called Giorgio.' Her voice wobbled and she rubbed her eyes. 'I met him five years ago, in a funny little village in the middle of nowhere in Italy. He spoke the local

24

dialect fluently but I knew he was English-born. There was something about his mannerisms – he hadn't mastered Italian gesticulation. It's hard to explain.'

'That doesn't mean anything. Lots of people look like other people.'

'Hear me out, Fi. Please. Giorgio – Gavin's ten years older than me. Maybe a bit more: one lie's much the same as another. But he's a charmer. Made me feel... Anyway.' She sniffed. 'I fell head over heels in love, we got married and settled in that funny little place and . . . I thought that was that.' She gazed at the shadowy form of Spetisham Hall. 'I never thought I'd settle down. It's why Simon and I didn't make it when we graduated: we wanted different things. But with Giorgio, it was different.'

'I'm sorry, Bianca,' said Fi, 'but I don't care about what you wanted or didn't want when you were twenty-one. I want to know what's going on now.'

'Don't you believe me?'

I don't want to believe you, thought Fi. *It can't be true.* 'This first photo was taken before you met Giorgio.'

'Yes,' said Bianca, snatching the photos. 'His mates in the *caffè* took it, long before I knew him. He told me to bring it because then you'd know it was him. The other one was taken a few months ago, before he – he—'

'Before he what?' Fi heard the sharpness in her voice, but didn't care. 'What's he been doing for fifteen years? If he has a nice little life in this funny little village and a pretty little wife, why risk spoiling it all by sending that pretty little wife to his old one, who'll tell the authorities and break his mother's heart?'

'Because . . . because he's ill.'

Fi blinked. Was she meant to feel sorry for him? *Did* she feel sorry? She yearned to look at the photographs again but Bianca had shoved them in her bag. 'How ill?'

'He needs an operation desperately. But there's a waiting list, and he— If they dig too deep, they'll find out Giorgio's living under a false name. He confessed everything to me. He'll have to go private. If he doesn't, he'll die.' Another deep sniff. 'He doesn't have any money – *we* don't. I thought we did. He made out we did. All these years I managed alone, and then I trusted him. But I found out—'

'It was all a front.'

'Yes.' Bianca's voice was a whisper. 'He said you'd tell me he did that to you too.'

Fi's stomach lurched and bile rose in her throat. 'I'm sorry about your husband,' she said, carefully. 'I'm not sure why you're telling me, though.' *Because it's Gavin*, said one part of her brain. *It can't be*, said another. *He's dead.*

26

'We all have lives we want to lead,' said Bianca. 'He made you miserable, didn't he? You don't want him back. His mother would never forgive him for lying: it might kill her. It's best she doesn't know. I love him, even if he lied to me, and I can make him the man he ought to be. I don't want him to die. *He* doesn't want to die. He said you'd help him with money for old times' sake, because you loved each other once. When he's well and on his feet, one day we'll repay you. I promise. He's a liar, but he's *my* liar.'

'If that first photo is really of Gavin and it was taken when you say,' snapped Fi, 'that was shortly after his girlfriend drowned and he was presumed drowned too. At home, his parents grieved and I struggled with the financial mess he'd left and the baby he'd abandoned.' Fi could hear her voice cracking. 'I didn't think Gavin was low enough to laugh in those circumstances. But I never really knew him, did I? You can't begin to imagine what I went through after he disappeared. If you're married to a man like that, you should run for the hills. Let me look at the photos again.'

Bianca stood up and rubbed her face with her hand. 'No. It's all right. I understand why you don't believe me. I won't bother you again. We'll find another way.' She ran along the gangplank and up the meadow towards the car park.

Fi didn't move. She *couldn't* move.

Her phone vibrated with a message from Jade. *Too tired to think. Bubbly sounds great. Thursday's better for drinks, but see you tomorrow for a chat. Hope you're having a lovely evening.*

Fi took her food below deck and threw it in the bin, then ran to the bathroom, where she was violently sick.

CHAPTER 4

Jade drove to Bertha's parking spot, fuming silently. 'Just' dropping Dylan off at Max's house had turned out to be less straightforward than anticipated. 'Where am I heading?' she had asked. She had to ask twice, because Dylan had his headphones in.

'Oh, sorry,' he said, when she nudged him. 'It's down there.'

'Down where?'

'It's through the alley, then left.'

'You may not have noticed,' said Jade, keeping her voice level, 'but Bertha won't fit in there. Know an alternative route? What street is it?'

'The one with the pub on the corner.'

'That narrows it down.'

Fifteen minutes later, after various three-point turns and reverses round the corner which reminded Jade of taking her driving test, they finally pulled up outside a house that Jade could have reached in two minutes with proper directions.

'Thanks, Jade,' said Dylan, getting out as if tomorrow would do. 'See ya!' He closed the door, not quite hard enough, and Jade had to unbuckle and slam it. *At least Hugo isn't a teenager any more. Though he might as well be, given the level of communication he's managed this weekend.*

When she had time, she had sent an occasional text asking how things were. She had received two replies: *Busy busy*, and *Fine*. A further enquiry had brought the message: *Don't fuss, Mummy. You're such a worrier.* That, of course, made Jade worry more.

She parked Bertha in her usual spot by the waste ground, hefted her bag, and locked up. *Hugo can fetch the box later. Or tomorrow morning.* She really wasn't bothered. *Fussing, indeed.*

The high street of Hazeby was still buzzing with bank-holiday cheer. Music came from several pubs and all the restaurants looked full. Jade eyed the chippy. Still open, and the queue wasn't long. *Good.*

She neared Crystal Dreams, and out of habit glanced at the shop window. Then she did a double take. Across the window, in curved, multicoloured lettering, was the legend *COME IN FOR BANK HOLIDAY BARGAINS!*

What did that mean? Jade peered in, but couldn't see much. She found her shop key and let herself in.

30

'What the—'

The shop looked as if it had been raided. Even the card racks were low on stock. And the shelves – not only were they practically empty, but they had moved. The little shelf where she put incense sticks and cones had shifted from near the till to beside the door.

Jade took out her phone and called Hugo. It went to voicemail. She texted: *What's going on in the shop?*

A reply came perhaps a minute later. *Welcome home, Mummy. We had a phenomenal weekend of sales. Check the fridge. Love, H x*

Why has everything moved?

This time, the reply was quicker. *I did some research.*

Oh no, she thought. She began to type a response, then deleted it. *You can tell me about it tomorrow.* She pressed *Send*.

Sorry, Mummy, meetings all day back at the ranch. Early start.

Jade huffed, scanned the shop and decided she didn't have the energy. *I'll ask Netta tomorrow.* She snapped off the light and went upstairs to her flat.

Stuck to the fridge door was a post-it note shaped like a cloud. *Open me!*

'Don't think you can get round me with food, Hugo,' Jade muttered. However, when she opened the fridge and found a bottle of white wine and a cheesy pasta bake labelled *Gas mark 6 for 15-20 minutes*, she reflected that things could be much worse. So long as Hugo and Netta hadn't swapped all her stock for a handful of magic beans.

***

Netta breezed in at ten to nine the next morning looking very pleased with herself.

'Someone had a good weekend,' said Jade. 'Did you and Hugo enjoy yourselves?'

'We worked so hard,' said Netta, putting her bag behind the counter. 'Hugo asked me lots of questions about what customers tend to buy and how many things at a time, and he said we had to increase our average cart value.'

'Our what?'

'The amount customers spend each time they visit,' Netta said patiently. 'He did what he said was a time and motion study and worked out that the average customer spends less than twenty pounds. He said we could double it by upselling.'

'Good grief,' said Jade. 'That doesn't explain why you've changed the shop round.'

'Oh yeah, Hugo did a thing called a heat map on Saturday morning and we rearranged the zones of the shop. With that, and the upselling, we made an average of thirty pounds per cart by the end of the day. That went up to thirty-five on Sunday.'

'You opened on Sunday? We never open on

Sunday.'

'We do on a bank-holiday weekend. Certainly from now on. And we did a special offer: a free pack of incense cones or sticks with every order over thirty pounds. So we need more stock. Did you bring anything back?' Netta looked at her like a dragon seeking to add to its hoard.

'One box,' said Jade.

Netta's jaw dropped. 'You took half the shop!'

'And I sold it. You weren't the only busy people.' Jade gazed around her depleted shelves. 'Make us a brew, will you, and I'll fetch the box. Then I can work out what to do.'

She opened the shop door to three people. 'Are the bank-holiday offers still on?' asked one.

Jade checked her watch. 'We open in five minutes, and then you can ask N— my assistant.' And off she strolled.

As she closed Bertha's boot and got a purchase on the box of stock, she pondered why she had said *assistant* instead of *Netta*. *You ought to be pleased*, she told herself. *You've wanted Netta to take the initiative for ages.*

She didn't, though. She was following Hugo's lead. While it may have worked this weekend – and I'll be going through the books – it may be a flash in the pan that turns out to be a damp squib. Whatever that looks like.

33

The box slipped and she rebalanced it. *Anyway, I'm not jealous. I've got nothing to be jealous about. I've sold a ton of stock this weekend and hopefully got us some new customers. Bringing in new footfall, that's where it's at.* And with a satisfied nod she walked back to the shop, taking her own sweet time.

The morning was comparatively quiet. Jade had expected that, after a bank-holiday weekend. Most people would be at work, nursing a hangover or possibly sunburn. It gave her the chance to tot up her takings, and the shop's. She was rather annoyed that Hugo and Netta had managed to pull in three hundred pounds more than she had, but then again, there was only one of her and she had left most of the expensive items in the shop. *If I'd had help, I'd have beaten them.*

On that pleasing note, she informed Netta that she had beaten them on per-employee income for the weekend and went to Betty's for Danish pastries. The size of the stock order she was about to put in required extra calories.

When she returned, Netta was serving a customer. 'I'm afraid we're out of *Change Your Life With Crystals*,' she said. 'However, we can put in an order and phone or text you once it's in. We had a very successful bank-holiday weekend.'

Do change the record, Netta, thought Jade. 'I'll make tea,' she said, and went into the back room. On the way, she passed a couple having an intensely murmured conversation behind the card rack. They broke off and watched her, but as she closed the back-room door the muttering resumed. *Honestly, people*, thought Jade, though she couldn't have said why it irritated her.

When she came out with two mugs of tea, Netta asked 'Can I take a break?' She yawned. 'I should probably have taken the day off, what with working on Sunday and Bank Holiday Monday.'

The words *I didn't ask you to work a three-day weekend* were on the tip of Jade's tongue, but she resisted. 'OK, why don't you take half an hour, have your usual lunch break, and go home early. We can work something out for the rest of the week.'

'Cheers.' Netta took her pastry from the bag on the counter, accepted her mug of tea, and wandered into the back room.

No rest for the wicked, thought Jade, taking Netta's place and opening the black notebook with the silver stars. *Time to run down that bank balance we've spent all weekend building up.*

'Excuse me?' The female half of the couple had emerged from behind the card rack. 'Do you know Fi Booker?'

'I do.' Jade found a fresh page and wrote a heading: *Post Bank Holiday Order*.

'I thought so,' said the woman, with a smile which

looked as if it was meant to be friendly but had turned out satisfied. 'Am I right in thinking that this is your shop?'

'It is.' *What are you, the shop police?*

Her smile broadened. 'Then you must be Jade Fitch.' She held out a hand and Jade felt obliged to shake it. 'I've read about you.'

'Only good things, I hope.' Jade took a draught of her tea, which was a bit too hot to drink comfortably. 'Are you looking for anything in particular? I'm afraid we're a bit low on stock this morning. It was a very busy bank-holiday weekend.'

'Oh, I'm sure it was,' said the woman. Her chin-length blonde curls bounced as she nodded. 'With a shop like this, I'm sure you sold loads. Fi probably did too.'

'I can't speak for Fi,' said Jade, 'but her shop does well. She works hard for it, as do I.' She tried not to think of Fi ambling round other people's stalls for half the weekend. At least, it had seemed that way.

'Of course,' said the woman. 'Fi has always fallen on her feet. First with that hotshot corporate job, and now this book boat.' Her nose wrinkled slightly.

'I take it you've known her for some time.'

'Oh yeah, we go waaay back. I was at her wedding.' The woman hooked her thumbs into the belt loops of her jeans and stood, foursquare.

'Uh-huh. Well, if you're planning to look Fi up,

she's returning today.' *She'll be delighted to see you*, Jade thought.

'Oh, has she been away?' the woman said, widening her pale-blue eyes.

Jade considered changing the subject, but Fi's participation in the festival at Spetisham Hall was common knowledge. And she was pretty sure the woman already knew. 'She's been at Spetisham Hall for a local festival, as have I.'

'Oh, silly me. Was she accompanied?' She giggled. 'If you know what I mean.'

'I stayed over on the boat, if that's what you mean.'

'Not you!' A roguish smile. 'Any . . . gentleman friends. I heard she was quite taken with a local policeman.'

'You seem to hear a lot,' said Jade. 'Now, is there something you wish to buy?'

'It's just a bit... What with her husband dying so tragically. It's a bit off to be canoodling with some chap she's known two minutes. Gavin would be spinning in his grave.'

'I doubt Gavin gives a monkey's,' said Jade. 'Just like when he left Fi with a young kid and a mountain of debt. And he's been gone for ten years or more. So I suggest you stop judging and leave Fi alone. She's worked hard to get back on her feet, and she doesn't need rumour-mongers bringing her down.'

The back-room door opened and Netta stuck her

head round it. 'Everything all right?'

'Oh yes,' said Jade. 'This customer is just leaving. We haven't got what she wants.'

'Can we order it in?'

'No,' snapped Jade. 'It isn't something we deal in.'

The woman's lip curled. 'If that's how you treat your customers, I'm surprised you get any. I was only passing the time before we go home tomorrow. Come on, Stefan.' She stalked to the door and her partner, a sheepish man in double denim, slunk after her.

'What happened there?' asked Netta, once they had left.

'I'm not sure,' said Jade. 'She seemed like a ghoul. And she wanted information about Fi.'

Netta's eyes widened. 'Will you let Fi know?'

'I probably should.' Jade took her phone from her skirt pocket and opened the messages app. *What can I say? Dear Fi, watch out for a woman who thinks you're the town floozy? Dear Fi, if a woman with short blonde curly hair comes to your boat, push her off with a boathook?* She put her phone on the counter. 'It'll only upset her. I'll leave it. Otherwise I'm spreading gossip, which is probably what *she* wants.' She took her Danish pastry from the bag and bit into it. But somehow, not even sugary pastry and apricot jam could cheer her.

CHAPTER 5

When Fi moored *Coralie* on Tuesday morning, for the first time she wished she were back in an office job where she could ring in sick and let someone else worry about the workload.

She'd sat for a while the previous evening, fingers poised over her phone, wondering what to say to whom. Jade was obviously asleep. Marcus was busy with work and hadn't replied to her earlier text till midnight. *Shift shocking. Bushed. Out of contact tomorrow unless urgent. Looking forward to Wednesday evening. XXX*

The moment when she could have told either of them about Bianca slipped away.

She'd slept fitfully. At dawn she woke, still trying to work out how Bianca could have found her, then cursed into the darkness. Of course: little snippets about Fi had got into the press after she and Jade had been involved in murder investigations. It was mostly inaccurate, but there must have been enough for Gavin to realise where she was, or—

'Gavin's dead,' she whispered to herself. 'Bianca read about me and being widowed, and because I live somewhere she once knew…'

She got out of bed and rooted around in the legal paperwork she'd had after Gavin's death. Though she couldn't find it, she recalled that during the period before he'd been presumed dead, a photograph much like the one she'd been shown had appeared in the press, asking for information.

It was that simple. A scanned photo, digitally improved, and a stock photo of a similar, older man. The only other thing Bianca needed was a criminal mindset. Perhaps that was the real reason she'd never settled down: she was a con artist.

Fi had been so shocked the previous evening that she'd never asked for Giorgio's surname, the name of the village in Italy, or any detail which might have corroborated the story. Bianca must have banked on that.

'Scammers everywhere,' she told Stan as she prepared to sail to Hazeby, knowing there was no hope of sleep. 'I bet even *you* think I'm an idiot. I don't want to tell Jade or Marcus that I almost fell for such a stupid trick.'

All the same, she considered telling Jade after both

shops were shut on Tuesday afternoon and they caught up over a cup of tea in Betsy's. However, Jade was wound up about something of her own.

'It's all heat and motion and time maps and basket value uplifting,' said Jade. 'I've been running businesses since the year dot without any of it. I'm livid!'

'Did the shop make a loss?'

'No, it made a profit. It's not good enough.'

Fi stared at her, eyebrows raised. 'You need another assistant and a holiday,' she said. 'I can see if Mum has any vacancies at her place in Normandy, if you like.'

'Not yet,' said Jade, darkly. 'I dread to think what will happen if I leave again.' She frowned. 'You look shattered. My customers were trying today. Were yours? Maybe it's the heat.'

'I had four complaints about *Coralie*'s lack of air-conditioning and Dylan is driving me nuts. What's the point of study leave? They might as well not revise at school as at home, when they're doing nothing else either.'

'Huh,' said Jade. 'Wait till he's reorganising your entire business plan.'

'Is that the one you have on the back of a postcard?'

'Cheek.' Jade grinned. 'I'll have you know it's on the back of an A4 envelope.' She checked her watch.

41

'Come round to mine on Saturday when there's no work the next day and we'll catch up properly. You bring that bottle of fizz you mentioned and I'll order a takeaway.'

Fi cleared her throat. 'I—'

Jade's phone rang. 'It's Hugo on FaceTime. Good: I can give him a piece of what's left of my mind. See you Saturday!' She gave Fi a quick one-armed hug, then marched out.

The following morning, Fi woke feeling even more ridiculous about not tackling Bianca. Business on the Book Barge was brisk – mostly parents buying emergency books to help their children revise. Fi felt like telling them it was a waste of money at this stage and was about to say so to Zach until she saw his gloomy expression. In a brief lull, she asked him what was wrong.

'I never got my exams,' he said. 'I'm such a dope.'

'You're not,' said Fi. 'You just didn't get the help you needed to snatch that first opportunity. It doesn't mean it's too late.'

'It is.'

'There's an open day at the college on Friday. Fancy going? They've got all sorts of courses for people who want to catch up. I can take you. I won't interfere, but if you need help with any questions I'll be there.'

'What about the shop?'

'We worked last Sunday. I'll shut for the day, or Dylan can run it. He could do with a rest from the revision he's not doing.'

Zach mused for a while. 'All right. But I'm paying for your lunch.'

After the shop closed, Fi dressed for her date with Marcus, said goodbye to Dylan, who was going to Alfie's, and took Stan for a walk. The riverside was busy with people, the river full of canoeists, paddle-boarders, and dogs and children splashing in the shallows. She and Stan walked under the bridge which Stan liked to visit most days, sniffing around for someone who was no longer there.

'Rrrerrfff?' Stan tensed and Fi followed where he was looking. A man was standing in the shade of a small tree. His face was stubbly, his hair greying. They stared at each other for a few seconds. It was the man from the photograph. Not a stock image: a real person.

'Coming through!'

From behind her, a trio of middle-aged male cyclists barrelled along the path, forcing Fi and Stan against the wall of the bridge. A group of female runners jogged in the cyclists' wake, chatting. The man slipped into their midst, then ran up the bank a few metres away.

Fi unfroze and ran after him, but he'd entered a patch of shrubbery and was climbing towards the road. By the time she'd scrambled through it, not only would she have ruined her clothes but he'd be up on the bridge, where he could go in either direction. Her nausea returned. Could he really be Gavin? She snatched Stan up and ran to *Coralie*. What should she do? She needed to find the original photograph. She needed to think. It had to be nonsense.

Marcus was waiting on deck for her. The smile on his face vanished as she approached. 'What's wrong? What's happened?' He reached for her but Fi held back.

'I – I—' *Oh, Marcus. I care for you so much and I don't know what to say.* 'I'm not feeling well.'

'You certainly look green. Is it something you ate? Let me get you some water.'

'No.' She put her hand on his arm. 'I need time to be alone and get over it. I'm sorry. I've ruined the evening.'

'I can play nursemaid,' said Marcus. 'I'm happy to mop your fevered brow.'

'No. Honestly. I might be sick.' She attempted a smile. 'I'd rather you didn't see that.'

'I wouldn't care.'

'Please? I'll ring tomorrow.'

Marcus hesitated, then sighed, his shoulders slumping. 'If you're sure. Message me later.'

'If I'm awake, I will. Promise.'

He kissed her cheek and she watched him walk

away, tears welling up. *What if I'm still married? What if I've been living a lie all these years? What if I can't see Marcus any more? What will I tell everyone? I can't think straight. Will Dylan believe I didn't know?*

Fi waited till he was out of sight then went below and sat at the table with her head in her hands, tears trickling through her fingers. It couldn't be true. If it was, why was Gavin lurking in bushes? Why hadn't he come with Bianca? *Be sensible, Fi*, she told herself. *Apply your brain logically.*

She collected paper and a pen to try and make sense of her thoughts, and had just started when there was a rap on the wheelhouse door. She tensed. Had Marcus returned? She half-hoped he had. Or was it the stranger?

'Hello?' The tentative greeting sounded familiar but it took her a moment to recognise it. Simon Davison. Had he brought Bianca? Fi called Stan to heel and went up to the wheelhouse.

Simon was alone, smiling in a friendly, open way, holding out a bottle of vintage burgundy and some roses. 'I hoped you'd be home. Sorry it's late, but I've got this gift from the Burlingtons and the Christmas Fayre has been confirmed, and I— Oh! Are you all right? You've, er, run a bit…' He circled his eyes with his fingers. Her mascara must have dissolved with the tears. So much for being waterproof. 'Hay fever?'

'It's that time of year,' said Fi. She was about to ask him to come back another time when she realised he could help. 'Bianca not with you? Where's she living these days?'

'She's sort of settled in Italy. Piedmont – is that right? But she's travelling round old haunts in the UK for a few weeks. She said she saw the fete advertised online and my name was mentioned, so she came. Serendipity!' His smile broadened. 'We're meeting on Friday for a late dinner. I mean, it's just a meal, but... Maybe she has contacts abroad. Maybe it's not too late to spread my wings.'

'It's never too late,' said Fi carefully. 'But don't rush into anything. So Bianca's here alone? Not with a friend or a significant other?'

'She hasn't mentioned anyone. Anyway, the Burlingtons would love you to be at the Christmas Fayre and I've suggested Jade brings Crystal Dreams to our autumn event. That seems more appropriate. Shall I email some dates when we could discuss logistics?'

'Yes, please,' said Fi. 'Thanks for these.'

As soon as he'd gone, she wiped the smeared mascara from her face and returned to her notes to add *Piedmont, date with Simon, no mention of husband*.

Her phone rang: an unknown number. She was about to refuse it on the assumption that it was a cold call but instinct made her change her mind.

'It's me, Bianca,' said the voice at the other end. 'Don't hang up.'

'How did you get my private number?'

'Simon.' Bianca sounded miserable. 'I told him I wanted to pick your brains about the bookshop.'

'You said you wouldn't bother me again.'

'I don't want to bother you. I want to explain. Can we meet?'

'Now?'

'No. I won't be back in Hazeby till Friday. I'm visiting my gran in York. She doesn't know who I am, but it may be the last time I'll see her.'

Fi wondered if this was true or another sob story. If it was true, why was the man from the photo wandering about without Bianca? 'I'll meet you on one condition,' she said. 'You bring Gavin or Giorgio or whoever he is. Actually, two conditions – the other is that you don't break Simon's heart. If you're really married, you have to let him down gently. He wants to rekindle things with you, and he's a nice man who doesn't deserve to find out he's being lied to.'

There was a brief silence. 'All right. Nine o'clock, at the riverbank entrance to the Old Manor pub. Do you know it?'

'Of course I do.'

'OK. Goodbye.' The phone went dead.

Right, thought Fi. *If I can face that, I can face*

Marcus. She messaged him. *I'm so sorry about earlier. Feeling a bit better now. Sorry if I ruined the evening.*

If you hadn't, I would have, came the reply. *I've had to go on duty. Acaster's off sick. I'll be tied up for a couple of days on a burglary. I'm sorry too. Must be fate. Rest up and get better soon.*

Fi's heart sank. She was ready to explain, but she couldn't do it by message. It had to be face to face.

Dots wibbled on the screen, then: *I'll be free Friday evening. Acaster should have regenerated by then.*

That'll be perfect, Fi replied. *Can you be here at 8.30? I'd like you to come somewhere with me.*

CHAPTER 6

'That's better,' said Jade, surveying Crystal Dreams with a smile. 'Finally, stock on the shelves.'

'I thought it was better as it was,' said Netta.

'What, with empty shelves and an out-of-date window display?'

'You know what I mean,' said Netta. 'The flow was good. And the window worked.'

'Yes, but it isn't a bank-holiday weekend any more,' Jade said, in what she felt was a very reasonable tone.

All in all, things had perked up since Tuesday evening, when she had met up with Fi. For one thing – and it was probably mean-spirited of her to think it – Fi wasn't her usual bright-eyed, bushy-tailed self. Probably the heat and tiredness from all that gallivanting, but it made Jade feel better about her weekend of beavering away.

Something she didn't have to feel guilty for taking pleasure in was that Fi hadn't mentioned any poisonous acquaintances dropping in for an impromptu visit. Maybe that woman was a false friend, the kind who was nice to your face and catty behind your back. She had seemed jealous of Fi, but in some ways that was understandable. Jade was, sometimes. But primarily Fi was her friend, whom she liked and trusted. Hopefully that woman would return to the swamp where she belonged. She hadn't even bought anything, the cheapskate.

And Hugo had finally got in touch. When Jade answered his FaceTime call as she left Betsy's, he was sitting on the sofa in the house he shared with a motley collection of student friends, resplendent in a pink paisley shirt, a navy cravat and a sports jacket. 'Hello Mummy, how are you?'

'Aren't you warm?' For a moment, Jade wondered whether the increase of traffic to Crystal Dreams over the weekend had been people visiting to see what on earth Hugo was wearing.

'I'm fine, and how are you? Do you like your new improved shop?'

'I'd like it better if you'd discussed it with me beforehand, rather than waiting till I was elsewhere to implement your grand plans.'

Hugo pouted. 'I take it that's a no.'

'I approve of the profit. Perhaps, once I've had a

chance to think about it, I'll approve of some of your ideas. But I'm surprised at Netta for letting you do it.'

'The window was her idea,' said Hugo. 'And the offer on the incense. She said you had loads and you could do with getting rid of some.'

Jade tried not to frown on camera. 'That wasn't the impression she gave me. From what she said, it was all down to you.'

Hugo shrugged. 'Netta has got more business smarts than you give her credit for. Maybe if you listened, instead of sending her to make tea and fetch bacon sandwiches—'

'I do my fair share of that! And while you two were playing shop and moaning about me, I was slaving away in the middle of a field!'

'Oh, Mummy.' Hugo looked contrite, but the corner of his mouth was twitching. 'We didn't moan at all. In fact, Netta said how much she likes working for you.'

'Oh. Good.'

Hugo laughed. 'You're such a drama queen. Anyway, would you consider keeping some changes and seeing how it goes? You can always put things back the way they were.'

'Maybe,' said Jade. 'Anyway, how are you and Netta getting on?'

'We're fine,' said Hugo. 'Um, do you know if she's seeing anyone at the moment?'

'If so, she hasn't mentioned it. Why, do you fancy your chances?'

'Very funny, Mummy. Actually, I asked her if she'd like to watch a film with me on Saturday night. There was an arthouse double bill at the local cinema, but she said she couldn't make it.'

'Mmm. I suspect that's down to your choice of film. Netta doesn't strike me as an arthouse type of person.' Jade considered. 'Is she *your* type of person?'

'I don't have a type of person, Mummy! Anyway, I'm glad you're home safely and not too angry about the shop.'

Jade smiled. 'I'll get over it. Thanks for coming over and holding the fort. I'll bear what you said in mind.'

'Oh yes, Mummy, I know what I wanted to ask you. Have you determined your customer avatar?'

'Good heavens, look at the time. Must dash. Goodbye, Hugo.' Jade ended the call and allowed herself a proper belly laugh. Customer avatar, indeed.

The next day, the first half of her stock order arrived mid-morning. Jim the delivery man grumbled as he brought in a box. 'What's in here, bricks?'

Jade inspected it. 'Cauldrons.'

Jim snorted. 'I suppose you've got brooms in the big one.'

'Haven't ordered any.' She grinned. 'Might be an

idea, though.'

'What will we do with brooms?' cried Netta.

Jade waited until Jim had gone out for another box before responding. 'I was pulling his leg. Now, can you unpack this and fill that shelf?' She pointed.

Netta's lower lip protruded slightly. 'We moved the cauldrons over there,' she said, pointing to the shelf by the window. 'We sell lots of them, so they're a draw. Then we put complementary items nearby, like measuring spoons and potion books. It's the cooking zone.'

Hugo's words floated into Jade's mind: *Maybe if you listened...* 'OK, that makes sense. Go on then.'

Netta looked both surprised and delighted. 'You don't mind?'

'Not if it's good for business. I'll get the kettle on. Maybe a cuppa will stop Jim from whingeing.'

Netta laughed. 'I don't think anything can stop Jim from— Oh, Jim, that's a big box. You must be very strong.'

A shy smile lit up Jim's weathered face. 'Got to be, in this job. Where do you want this one? And just to warn you, there's another five in the van.'

After three cups of tea and a protracted period of negotiation, Jade had conceded a few points. The window display was a little more brightly coloured – teal and turquoise instead of purple and black – to reflect the warm weather. The shelves were less crammed with items, allowing customers to see the stock better. And Jade had approved the placement of the card rack near the front of the shop. She was sick of watching people lurking behind it.

However, business was quiet. Obviously, or they would never have had time to make the changes. 'It's midweek,' said Netta. 'And people probably spent loads on bank-holiday weekend, so they're out of cash.'

'Doesn't normally bother them,' said Jade.

In addition, two of the three witches had come in and looked rather nonplussed as they gazed around the shop. 'You've moved things,' said the first witch, fingering her silver four-leaf clover pendant as if for reassurance.

'Yes,' said Jade. 'We're trying something new. What do you think?'

A tiny wrinkle appeared between the second witch's eyebrows. 'It's . . . not bad, but I don't see why. I knew where everything was before.'

Jade shot Netta a triumphant glance. 'We can always change it back. We're keen to act on customer feedback.'

And so, when the rest of Jade's order came on Thursday, changes were made.

'They'd have got used to it,' Netta said sulkily, as she hung more silver charms on the hooks.

'They might have,' Jade replied. 'It was too much

change in one go. I kept a few things, anyway. Maybe if we make one or two changes at a time it'll be less startling.'

'Can I take a break?' said Netta. 'I feel as if I've been lugging boxes all day. And we haven't sorted out my time back for the long weekend.'

'That's true. Go on, take a long lunch hour. I've got a sandwich, so I'll hold the fort until half two.'

'OK.' Netta got her bag and left.

Jade sighed. She could see why Netta was in a mood, but she couldn't afford to lose business because of Netta and her son's highfalutin theories. *It has to work in the real world*, she told herself.

The door creaked. 'That was quick,' she said.

'Only me,' said Rick.

'Oh. Hi.'

She hadn't spoken to Rick since Monday, at Spetisham Hall. It wasn't that they had fallen out, more that she didn't want him to think she was hanging round him now that Shelley had, presumably, gone home to write up her research.

'I wondered if you fancied going out for lunch.' He looked around. 'Netta not in?'

'She's on a long lunch today, so I'm eating at my desk.'

'Oh, OK. Tomorrow, maybe?'

'Fridays are normally busy. As are Saturdays.'

'All right, what about a drink after work?'

What's got into you? 'Yeah, if you like. I could do with letting my hair down, what with Shop Wars. Shelley get off all right?'

'Yeah, I dropped her at her boyfriend's.'

'She's got a boyfriend?'

He laughed, his eyes crinkling at the corners. 'It happens.'

'Don't you mind?'

'Nooo. When we split up, we both said we wanted to stay friends. Friends don't get jealous of other people's new partners.'

Jade sniffed. 'You're very free and easy.'

Rick smiled. 'I take it you haven't stayed friends with any of your exes, then.'

'None of your business,' Jade snapped.

Rick took a step back. 'I'm sorry if I touched a nerve.'

'You didn't. I'm fine.'

'OK.' He paused, looking at her. 'Well, if you do want to go for a drink tonight, I'll be in the Swan from eight.'

'Uh-huh. I'll see how it goes. I'm still a bit tired from the weekend.'

'Maybe see you later, then.' Rick raised a hand and ambled out.

For something to do, Jade went to the back room, put her sandwich on a plate to make it a bit more fancy, and took it to the counter. She contemplated it, her mind far away. What was Rick getting at? Was he trying to find out about her previous relationships? Or was he lonely now that Shelley had gone home? And how could you stay friends with an ex? Then again, if you stayed clear of relationships, that was less of a problem. Men were just trouble, on the whole, and the less of that she had to put up with, the better.

She took a bite of her sandwich and made a face. She'd skimped on the butter and the bread was sticking to the roof of her mouth. *Ugh*, she thought, and went to make yet another cup of tea.

CHAPTER 7

As it turned out, Fi didn't have to close the Book Barge on Friday. After the fete, Nerys had taken a few days off to spend with her children before the eldest started preschool, so she offered to run things while Fi went to the college open day with Zach. Her one proviso was that she'd like Dylan to help.

Dylan muttered darkly that if he failed because of a day's missed revision it would be Fi's fault. Fi pointed out that Nerys would only call him when it got busy and if he liked, she'd test him when it was quiet.

Dylan rolled his eyes.

'You'll get paid.'

'I'd better.'

Zach arrived at five to ten, dressed in a plain white shirt and black jeans with his hair styled, and clearly nervous. 'All right, Dylan? You don't know how lucky you are to get this done now. I'm going to feel a right numpty, three years late.'

Dylan had the grace to look a little ashamed of his earlier belligerence, not that there was any hope of an apology. 'You'll be fine, mate,' he said. 'You can explain bits of maths better than my maths teacher. It's like you know it by instinct.'

'Yeah, but—'

'You won't be the oldest by a mile, Zach,' said Fi. 'Trust me. And relax. It's not like school, and there's more than one thing to go for. Not just exam subjects, but apprenticeships with college day release.'

'I like the shop,' he said, 'and the numbers and the accounts. It's weird, but . . . I like facts being tidy.'

'There'll be plenty to choose from that'll fit in with that,' said Fi. 'Let's go.'

'Good luck,' said Dylan, giving him a thumbs up.

The open day went well. As she'd predicted, there were plenty of courses and apprenticeships for Zach to enquire about, and his confidence grew the more people he talked to. It was a shame that Simon Davison wasn't there to explain how Spetisham Hall worked with the college, partly because she wanted to pick his brains and also because she felt she should drop a subtle hint about not trusting Bianca. But the hall's stand was run by his young female assistant, who told Zach about event planning and administrative opportunities.

By mid-afternoon it became clear that Zach no longer needed Fi, so she found the refreshments section and sat down to scroll through her phone. It had been good to have something to take her mind off things, but now her worries were crowding back in.

The previous day had been torture: more than once, Fi had thought of asking one of her friends for advice. But it felt wrong not to talk to Marcus first. She'd considered sending him a voicemail and wondered if she ought to report Bianca's request for money as a possible crime, or report the man who looked like Gavin as loitering on the towpath, though she hadn't seen him since. The more she thought about it, the more it felt as if she was being played. She wanted to know what had made Bianca target her. If Bianca was telling the truth and the man *was* Gavin, Fi wanted to have it out with him in private before she had him arrested. Not that she was sure what he'd be arrested for.

After she came home and the shop was closed, Fi prepared an early dinner and got ready for what lay ahead. There was no point getting dressed up. Marcus might walk away once she told him, or she might have to chase the man through the shrubbery. So she put on jeans and an old T-shirt and left her face unmade up, then went to tidy the shop.

'What's up, Mum?' said Dylan.

Fi shook herself. 'Up? What? I mean, what do you

mean?'

'You didn't eat much and now you're fussing like a . . . fussy thing. You haven't heard anything I've said, have you? And you're always complaining about me not listening to you.'

'I'm sorry.' Fi sat down at the table. 'Things on my mind.'

'You and Marcus split up?'

'No. Why would you think we had? And we're not exactly serious.'

'Oh come on, Mum. Not that I mind, exactly. He's OK, for a copper.'

'What have you got against the police?'

'Nothing. But Leo says it's a right pain having one for a dad. He's never around, for a start. I know what that's like, don't I?' His jaw clenched. 'What if Dad hadn't died? Would he have been around?'

Fi hesitated, looking into those eyes that were so like Gavin's within a face so different. She couldn't answer. She'd always thought Gavin would have been one of those fathers who appear from time to time and shower their children with gifts, junk food and expensive activities, leaving the mundane to the mum – as well as the fallout from broken promises. 'I hope so,' she said.

'Meh.' Dylan shovelled in the last mouthful of pasta and stood up. 'I'm going out.'

'Er, where to?' What if Dylan and whoever he was

with decided to walk along the river towards the Old Manor?

'I *told* you. I knew you weren't listening. Aren't I allowed? Are you making me *revise* now, when you've made me work all day?'

'Of course you're allowed: I just wondered where you were off to. I'm going for a walk by the river with Marcus.'

Dylan pulled a face. 'Thanks for warning me: I don't want to see old people snogging. I'm going to the pictures. Don't fall in.'

Moments after he'd gone, Marcus rang. 'I'm sorry, I can't make it,' he said. 'Something's come up.' His voice was stern and a little distant. 'Can you manage whatever it is without me?'

'I… I really did want you.'

'You didn't the other night.'

'But—'

'Honestly, I can't come and I can't explain why.' Marcus let out a sigh. 'Stay safe, Fi. I've got to go. See you as soon as I can. I— Just stay safe.'

She sat for a moment, staring at the phone. Had she annoyed him that much the other evening? Or was it what Leo had told Dylan: a police officer isn't around much and she'd have to get used to it? But he'd sounded so cold.

This is ridiculous, she told herself. *I've got to face her – them – but I can't go alone. Jade will kill me for not trusting her, but… Maybe she'll take out her fury on Bianca instead. At least she'll be a witness.*

Ten minutes later, she and Jade walked along the river while Fi gave her a brief summary of what had happened on Monday evening. Most of the sky was the same apricot colour, with streaks of white trailing across the darkening blue. The riverbank was empty but for Fi and Jade. It was an evening for walking hand in hand with a lover, not pouring out secrets to an irritated friend and preparing to face your fears – and possibly your enemy.

'So you kept this bottled up for a whole week because…?' said Jade, stopping and folding her arms.

'I wanted to tell Marcus first. If I'm still married, I'm not free to go out with him. I'm being unfaithful and doing to Gavin what he did to me, and—'

Even in the dusk, it was possible to make out Jade's eyes rolling. 'It's not even *close* to being the same. If Gavin's alive, he's even more of a lying, stinking, cheating coward than you thought. And if Marcus were here, with any luck he'd punch him, police code or no police code. Now it'll have to be me. I wish you weren't so secretive.'

'You're one to talk.'

'Huh.' Jade started walking again. 'It's not the same. Anyway, once we get this over with, you owe me a large glass of wine. '

'Don't joke.'

63

'I'm not. I've had a week of regaining Crystal Dreams from a hostile takeover bid and I'm just in the mood to deal with a scheming trollop and a Gavinalike.'

'Shh. We're nearly there.'

They walked in silence for a while. Fi could feel her heart hammering and hugged herself. They turned the last bend in the bank and she watched her feet take one step in front of another towards who knew what.

'Hang on,' said Jade. 'Is there a do on at the Old Manor?'

'What?'

'Look through the trees. It's not very welcoming, though.'

Bright white light blinded Fi and she stumbled. They were almost at the place where she was meant to meet Bianca. She heard voices, serious and low. Surely Bianca hadn't brought a gang? Surely— She walked straight into blue and white plastic tape closing the path. 'What the—'

Ahead, she could make out five or six figures at the water's edge, silhouetted against the light. Two were bending. 'Over here, sir.'

'Sir?' whispered Jade. 'What's going on?'

'Her dress is caught on something, sir. She'd have been swept off downstream then sunk else. No one would have found her for weeks. Years, maybe.'

'Oh my goodness,' said Fi, swallowing.

'It's a boathook, sir. It's caught her skirt then got wedged in the bank.'

'More photos in situ, please.' It was Marcus's voice.

Flash, flash, flash.

'Right, can you get her out? Carefully, in case there's a chance.'

'Don't reckon there's a snowball's chance in a furnace, sir, but we'll be careful.'

There was a sickening, sucking, sloshing sound. The silhouettes lifted first a boathook, then a rigid female body from the water. A long skirt and strands of hair dangled before they laid her gently on the ground.

'Reckon someone pushed her in with the boathook,' said a woman's voice. 'Doesn't look accidental.'

'That's for the pathologist to determine, sergeant,' said Marcus.

'Don't recognise her,' said a man's voice. 'Tourist, maybe? We need a handbag or a phone or some kind of ID, else it'll be a job and a half to find out who she is.'

'I know,' called Fi.

Everyone looked over. A figure strode forward, becoming Marcus. 'Fi? What the—'

'If it's who I think it is, she's called Bianca

Spencer and she's from Italy.'

'How do you know that?'

'Because I arranged to meet her here and I'm ten minutes late. How long has she been dead?'

CHAPTER 8

Marcus looked at Fi for some time without speaking. His face wore the neutral expression that, to Jade, meant trouble. Eventually, he cleared his throat. 'We don't know that yet.' He turned. 'Sergeant Blake, you're needed.' He faced them again. 'Ms Fitch, could you please accompany Ms Booker while Sergeant Blake asks some questions?'

'Umm…' Jade's mind was whirling. 'Does Fi have to do that now? She's probably in shock.'

'I'm fine,' said Fi, quietly. 'So I might as well get it done.'

'OK,' said Jade. 'But you can stop whenever you want.'

'If you'd like to come this way,' said Sergeant Blake, leading the way to a bench further down the path. 'Please take a seat. Sorry to loom over you.' He pulled a notebook from his pocket. 'I'm afraid we'll have to be formal. Ms Booker, you have suggested the deceased may be a Bianca Spencer. Could you tell me why you think that?'

'Remember, Fi, you can stop whenever you want,' said Jade.

Fi stared at the river for a few moments, then sighed. 'I met Bianca Spencer a few days ago, during the festival at Spetisham Hall. She was introduced to me by Simon Davison, the events manager. We chatted for a little while and she was interested in the Book Barge. I thought nothing of it until she came to visit me again on Monday evening...'

As she continued the narrative, Jade gave her a warning look, then coughed. But Fi continued to talk. It was as if she was determined to get it all out.

'You had arranged to meet here this evening?'

'Yes,' said Fi. 'I was a bit late, as I was filling Jade in. I asked her to come at the last minute because I wanted to have someone with me. Mar— Inspector Falconer was meant to accompany me, but he was called away. He doesn't know any of this. I was going to tell him tonight.' She twisted her hands in her lap. 'That probably makes me sound guilty as anything, doesn't it? But I didn't do it. So who did?'

'That's what we're here to find out,' said Sergeant Blake, making a final note and closing his notebook.

'Fi, are you sure that was this Bianca woman?' asked Jade. 'We were a few metres away and you've seen her, what, twice?' *Talk about shutting the stable door after the horse has bolted,* she thought. *Why didn't you ask that fifteen minutes ago, before Fi started talking?*

'I think so,' said Fi. 'The clothes were right – I've seen Bianca in a similar dress – and the hair was the right length and colour. No one else recognised her, so she isn't local. But I could have jumped to conclusions because she was the person I expected to see. Not dead,' she added hastily. 'On the riverbank with her – her husband. If he is her husband. Could I look more closely?'

'I'm afraid not,' said Sergeant Blake. He reopened his notebook and scribbled another note, then flipped it shut. 'Ms Booker, is your son at home tonight? You've had a shock, and you should probably have someone with you.'

Fi shook her head. 'He's at the cinema, then staying over with a friend.'

Sergeant Blake looked at Jade. 'In that case... Ms Fitch, am I right in thinking you live quite close?'

'Yes, I'm about ten minutes' walk from here.'

'In that case, would you mind taking Ms Booker home with you? Or taking her to her boat and sitting with her. Whatever's convenient.'

'That's fine,' said Jade. 'Come on, Fi, let's go.' She got up and held out a hand to Fi. More than anything, she wanted to get Fi away from the police and the

69

scene.

Fi got slowly to her feet and brushed down her jeans.

'Oh, Ms Booker...'

'Yes?'

'We may need to visit and take a more formal statement at a later date. And we must ask you to stay in Hazeby.'

'Is that necessary?' asked Jade.

'I'm afraid it's official policy,' said Sergeant Blake, pocketing his notebook. 'I don't have any say in the matter. I'm sorry.'

Fi set off along the riverbank and Jade had to stride to catch up. She waited for Fi to start shaking, or crying, or . . . something, but she just carried on walking. 'Do you want to talk?' Jade asked, after a while.

'Not really. I've said all there was to say. I was going to tell Marcus tonight. I would have told him before, but... Things happened. Now he'll hear it through Sergeant Blake's notebook.' Fi spoke as if it was happening to somebody else, a long way away.

'I'll take you back to mine,' said Jade. 'Unless you want to go to *Coralie*?'

'I don't mind,' said Fi. 'It doesn't matter.' And she continued to walk in silence.

Jade paced beside her, cursing herself for not thinking quickly enough. She should have turned round when they saw the bright light and the police officers, not gone to see what it was. She should have refused to let them question Fi, or said *Not without a lawyer*. Fi was in no state to act in her own best interests.

They were back in Hazeby's high street a few minutes later. It was noisy with Friday-night music and laughter which made Jade clench her teeth. 'Not far now,' she said, for something to say.

'You don't have to put me up,' said Fi. 'I can walk home in a bit.'

'I'll worry about that later.' Jade pulled out her keys, ready to get them into the flat as soon as possible.

Luckily, she'd left it in a reasonable state. Not that Fi cared. She sat on the sofa, gazing through the opposite wall.

'Tea? Or something stronger?'

'Tea is fine,' said Fi. 'I'm not in the mood for alcohol. And I should probably keep a clear head.'

Jade filled the kettle and switched it on. 'You didn't have to tell them absolutely everything.'

'I could have said nothing and left them to work out who she was. But *he's* still out there. While he is, I'll have no peace.' She pulled a cushion to her and hugged it. 'Besides, what if I said nothing, then he came forward to identify the body and told them about me? That would look a thousand times worse.'

71

'If he *is* Gavin,' said Jade. 'I thought you were sure it was a moneymaking scam.'

'I'm not sure of anything any more.'

The kettle pinged. Jade made tea, put the two mugs and a packet of chocolate Hobnobs on the coffee table, and sat next to Fi, who continued to stare into space. After a couple of minutes, Jade opened the packet. Fi didn't move.

'I'll put the TV on low, for background noise.'

'OK.'

'Tell me if you want to talk.'

Jade flicked through the channels, rejecting a police car-chase show and *Great Canal Journeys* for a cookery programme. Then she realised it was set in Italy, and channel surfed until she found an old edition of *Top Of The Pops*. Suddenly, Fi stared at the screen. 'The DJ played that at our wedding,' she said.

Jade turned off the TV just as someone rang the doorbell. 'I'll get that,' she said. 'It's probably Rick. No one else would come round at this time.'

He wouldn't, either.

She opened the door to Marcus Falconer. 'What a pleasant surprise.'

'I tried *Coralie* first,' he said. 'I assume Fi's with you. I need a word. May I come in?'

'Don't suppose I can stop you,' said Jade, and opened the door wider. 'Be as nice as you can,' she murmured. 'I know you're a cop, but she's having a rough, rough time.'

His expression conveyed nothing. 'Upstairs?'

'Yes.'

Jade trailed upstairs behind him, wishing she could go first and warn Fi. Marcus waited at the top of the stairs for her, which was something. 'You should probably tell her it's me,' he muttered.

Jade went past him and into the flat. 'Marcus is here,' she said.

Fi put the cushion back on the sofa. 'OK.'

Jade went to the door and beckoned Marcus in. 'Remember what I said.'

Marcus walked into the living room and glanced around for a chair. There was only the sofa, so he remained standing. 'I'm sorry to have to come in an official capacity. I won't stay long, but I need a little more information if you can give it. First of all, are you missing a boathook? I assume you have one on the barge.'

Fi looked up at him. 'I do have one, but I couldn't say if it's missing. I haven't used it since I moored *Coralie* on Tuesday morning.'

'Did you put it away in its usual place?'

'It doesn't get put away, exactly. It's kept on the deck on the far side of the wheelhouse, where customers can't trip over it.'

'So potentially, anyone could take it?'

'I suppose so.'

Finally, something positive, thought Jade.

'It's highly likely that we'll have to search your boat,' said Marcus. 'Will it be necessary for me to obtain a warrant?'

Fi's eyebrows drew together. 'Of course not. If it's important, we'll go now.' She stood up.

'That won't be—'

'I said we can go now,' snapped Fi. 'I should go home anyway, and it may as well be now as later.'

'I'll come with you,' said Jade. 'I can stay the night if you like.'

'I have a car downstairs,' said Marcus. 'My car, not a police car.'

After a few minutes for Jade to get some things together and Marcus to make a phone call, they walked downstairs. Marcus opened the rear passenger door. Fi gave him a long look, then got in. Jade followed. She wanted to give Fi a hug, but she sat so rigidly that Jade thought she might break.

Marcus parked at the top of the cobbled walkway which led to the towpath. 'I've asked Sergeant Blake to meet us there.' Jade saw a uniformed figure standing by the gangplank.

'Will you search the whole boat?' asked Fi.

'Just the deck, for the boathook. You're sure that's where you left it?'

'Yes.'

'You only have one boathook?'

'Yes.'

'Yes, she does,' said Jade, though she had no idea.

They followed Marcus down to the boat. He had a brief conversation with Sergeant Blake. 'We'll go on deck, if that's all right.'

'It's fine,' said Fi. She sounded weary.

'Do you want to go inside?' Jade asked.

'Not while they're there.'

The men switched on torches and patrolled the boat, the beams moving like miniature searchlights. A few minutes later, they came to the side of the boat. 'Could we come in for a few minutes?' asked Marcus.

Fi crossed the gangplank and let them in. 'Tea?'

'That won't be necessary,' said Marcus.

They stood in the main part of the boat, awkward amongst the bookshelves and the displays. 'I take it you didn't find the boathook,' said Fi.

Marcus shook his head. 'We didn't. Can you tell me whether your boathook has any distinguishing marks? An unusual hook, or damage, or a label…'

'Yes, it does,' said Fi. 'When I first came here, people kept borrowing my boathook and forgetting to return it. I started carving the boat's name on the handle, but my penknife broke. So it says COR halfway down the handle.' And a shadow passed over Marcus's face.

CHAPTER 9

With nothing to lose, and perhaps some credibility to gain, Fi asked Marcus and Sergeant Blake to do a cursory search of *Coralie*'s shop and living quarters. Not that anyone who'd stolen the boathook would have needed to come inside. She hoped they had never been inside, under any circumstances.

As they prepared to leave, Marcus offered to shake hands as if he was a mere acquaintance.

'Ooh, Sergeant Blake – I heard a noise on the deck!' said Jade. 'I'm sure it's safe to go and check.' She made for the steps.

'Better wait for me, Ms Fitch.' The sergeant hurried after her, leaving Fi and Marcus alone.

'I wish you'd messaged about Bianca on Monday,' said Marcus, maintaining the handshake longer than socially normal.

'I wanted to talk face to face.'

'You could have talked on Wednesday, but you pushed me away.'

'I needed to process everything. At least I've told you now. I could easily have told you nothing when I saw you pull that woman from the water. And poor Simon will be waiting for her to turn up for their date. Horrible as it is to say, I think he's had a lucky escape.'

'Assuming the body is Bianca Spencer's,' said Marcus. 'I hope Simon can give us details of someone who can identify her formally – a relation, perhaps. Otherwise he'll have to do it himself. That seems harsh, since they've only just reconnected. But maybe the body will be someone else entirely and we'll be seeking Bianca Spencer for attempted fraud.' He almost smiled, then became grave again.

Fi wondered if he was thinking of the possibility that Bianca had been telling the truth about Gavin, and connecting it to the boathook.

'I wanted you to be with me this evening when I met her,' she said. 'Because you couldn't, I took Jade. I'd hardly take a witness if I was going to kill someone. Not that I'd kill someone *without* a witness. And I didn't need to tell you anything about her, or the visit on Monday. Surely you don't think—'

'No,' said Marcus, releasing her hand. 'But I don't think my views count for much. Not even to you, as you didn't tell me any of this. Besides… No, I can't.'

'Can't what?'

'Wrong time. For official, not personal reasons. I'll explain when I can.'

'You don't know what it was like, having Bianca say that.'

'No, I don't. But I know what it is to listen without judgement.'

'Is that what you're doing?'

'Trying to. Don't get in touch with me: it'll look odd. I'll get in touch with you when I can. Now I'd better speak to Simon Davison, then see if Acaster's well enough to take over.'

'I don't want—'

'Nor do I. But it may not be our choice.'

Once the police had gone, Fi told Jade she'd be all right alone. 'Stan and I will walk you to the first streetlight. Stan will protect us if we need it.'

'What will he do?' said Jade, reluctantly crossing the gangplank. 'Snuffle people to death?'

'He growled at the man in the bushes.'

'The Gavinalike? He was meant to be meeting you too. So where is he now? Is he at the bottom of the river, did *he* kill her, or...' Jade slowed. 'Fi, are you sure that woman was Bianca?'

'Not certain. It was a general impression, a feeling, and—'

'And the fact that she was where you were supposed to meet her. What if it's not Bianca, but someone else?'

'That's what Marcus hinted at.'

'I'll bet he did,' said Jade. 'What if Bianca or the Gavinalike killed some random woman, thinking it was you?'

'That body was nothing like me – shorter, long hair, bustier—'

'The sun was setting. It's easy to make mistakes in the dark. I'm coming back to the boat with you.'

'No you're not,' said Fi. 'You've got a shop to look after. I'll be all right.'

Jade made a noise more frightening than Stan's growl. 'OK. I know when I'm not wanted, but I'll keep my phone on. Put trip hazards on your deck. And don't go back and wallow in self-pity. Marcus won't let anything be pinned on you.'

'He might not talk to me ever again, either.'

'If he gives you the silent treatment for more than a few days, he's not worth wasting tears over,' said Jade.

'I'm not crying.'

'Good.'

And Fi didn't cry. But she lay awake for hours, wondering what she'd done to deserve her love life falling apart every time she thought she'd found someone worth falling in love with. She didn't think the police – even Inspector Acaster, if she took charge – would pin anything on her, but the evidence wasn't great. She didn't know what Bianca had told Simon, or how he might have interpreted it.

She got up early and trawled through albums and her computer for photos of Gavin from around the time he'd left her. There weren't many, and in none of them did he look like someone who would murder. Manipulate, yes. Lie, yes. Control, yes. Violence? Perhaps it was just one more step for someone who always wanted his own way.

Morning brought Dylan home early enough for breakfast. He seemed pensive.

'Film good?' asked Fi, with no idea what it had been, but not in the mood to be criticised for some infinitesimal infringement on teenage boundaries.

'Great,' said Dylan. 'But when we came out, someone said something had happened a mile downriver. Blue lights and an ambulance. Did you go for your walk with Marcus last night? Or was he busy?'

Fi hesitated for a second. She didn't want to give Dylan reason to think that she was a liar if it turned out that somehow, Gavin was alive. 'He was busy. If I tell you something, you have to keep it quiet for a bit, agreed? Not even tell Max or Alfie or Chloe.'

'Deal.' Dylan frowned. 'Did a bloke go in the river?'

'Why a bloke, in particular?'

'Dunno. They do sometimes when they've had one

too many.'

'Oh, I see. No, but when Jade and I went for a walk, we saw the police take a woman's body from the river.'

'Drowned?'

'I don't know. But she's dead. The police aren't releasing any details, but they wanted to know where our boathook was.'

'*Our* boathook?' Dylan went pale. 'Isn't it in its place?'

'Apparently not. I thought I should tell you, in case anyone saw them looking for it last night.' She sighed. 'The other liveaboards may have seen something.'

'But it's nothing to do with us, is it?'

'I hope not,' said Fi. 'Don't say anything till it's public, all right?'

'Yeah.' Dylan went to make more toast. 'Look, Mum… I know I've got it easier than Zach, but I *am* revising. Honest. I'm just doing it my own way, OK?'

'I—'

'I'm not you. I'm me. It's not the nineteen hundreds any more, like when you did GCSEs.'

'Nineteen nineties.'

'Same difference,' said Dylan. 'Either way, exams are pointless but I *am* revising.'

Fi rubbed her eyes, too tired and stressed to argue. 'Sadly, no one has worked out an alternative. You do you, Dylan. Just don't push your luck.'

Her phone vibrated. 'Oh crikey, it's Nana.' Her finger was poised to answer. But what would her mother-in-law say? Was the murder public knowledge already? Had the news got onto national websites? If it had, Annie would be fussing about Dylan. If it hadn't, what if Gavin was alive and he'd gone to see her? Fi couldn't even begin to imagine the fallout.

She answered just before the call went to voicemail, trying to sound cheerful and carefree. 'Hi, Annie, you're early! Is everything all right?' She expected Dylan to call out a greeting but he sat listening, his toast half-buttered.

'Perfectly fine, thank you,' said Annie. 'I wondered if you and Dylan would like to come round on Sunday. You must be shattered after working last weekend and Dylan probably needs a rest from revising. You shouldn't make him do it. Gavin hardly needed to revise at all.'

Gavin was a lucky chancer, thought Fi. *Stuffed his brain the night before, regurgitated it in the exam, then forgot it.* 'Nana thinks you're revising too much,' she told Dylan.

Dylan's smile returned and he started buttering again. 'Too right!'

'Yes, we'd love to come,' said Fi. 'I appreciate it.' At least it would be easy to find photographs of Gavin at his mother's house. She pushed down the thought that the police might have other plans for her if they misunderstood what she'd told them.

But surely Marcus wouldn't let that happen. She checked her phone over and over again as she got the boat ready for customers, but there was nothing. The dead woman wasn't in the online news, either.

At ten to nine Zach arrived, waving a brochure. 'I had a chat with Mum and her mate, and a kid I knew at school – a sensible one – and… I'll give it a go.'

'That's great news,' said Fi. 'What were you thinking?'

'If I sign up for the right apprenticeship, the college will help me get English and Maths to make up for not having GCSEs. I fancy tourism and business, with digital marketing. I could help you with your website, if I can borrow your old laptop—' His face fell. 'I suppose you won't want to let me. I wouldn't be here two days a week…'

'The scheme would help me, too,' said Fi, hoping that were true. 'Even if it doesn't, I'd be delighted to have your help with the website. It's really not my cup of tea.'

'Phew.' Zach grinned and put down the brochure. 'You're a star. Oh, here's your post.' He handed over a bundle of envelopes, then he and Dylan went to set up the upper-deck shop.

Fi flicked through the post. The third letter was in the kind of plastic envelope secondhand books sometimes came in, addressed with a printed adhesive label. But there was no book inside, just a letter. It had been written in pencil using a stencil: every letter was formed in the same way. It looked as if it had been written by a child, but the words were anything but childish.

Bianca was killed with your boathook. You had everything to lose if she went public with what she knew. Your squeaky clean reputation, your shop, your son's love and maybe his future career.

Bianca wasn't the only one to know the truth. I know more than she did. Even the stuff you've never told anyone.

You can afford the money to keep me quiet. Wait for more instructions. And if you tell the police – even your nice boyfriend – you'll lose everything in the worst possible way.

Fi's hand started to shake. She should tell Marcus. But he'd ask what the letter meant about *the stuff you've never told anyone* and she had no idea. Besides, he'd told her not to contact him.

'You look a bit peaky, Mum,' said Dylan, as he came down for a box of books. 'Perhaps you need a coffee.'

'You're dead right,' said Fi, rolling her shoulders, standing up straight and picking up her phone. 'And I'm going to have one with Jade.'

CHAPTER 10

Jade was in the middle of a 'discussion' with Netta when her phone buzzed. 'Hang on a minute,' she said, and fetched it from the counter.

It was a text from Fi. *Could you spare time for a brew? Betsy's in 10 minutes?*

Jade considered. The current discussion, about increasing basket value, was making her lose the will to live. While there was a strong possibility that Netta would implement some of her ideas while Jade was out of the shop, she wasn't sure that was such a bad thing. Her case against it was on distinctly shaky ground. *Sure*, she replied.

Great, see you soon x

Hmm, thought Jade. Fi wasn't a habitual x-er. She turned to Netta, who was drawing a breath to launch another key point. 'I need to pop out for a bit,' she said. 'Are you OK to hold the fort?'

'I suppose,' said Netta, but she was finding it hard not to smile.

Jade was heading out of the shop when she nearly walked into Rick. 'Steady on,' he said, half-laughing.

'Sorry, I'm in a hurry.'

'Oh.' He deflated slightly. 'I was on my way to ask if you fancied a drink tonight.'

'In the Swan? Why not.' It might distract her from worrying about Fi. She could always cancel if this meeting yielded new information.

'We could go to Ritzy's wine bar.'

Jade goggled at him. 'We always go to the Swan.'

Rick shrugged. 'A change is as good as a rest, they say.'

'Oh. OK.' *What's brought this on?*

'Anyway, I'll let you go if you're in a hurry,' said Rick. 'I'll call for you at eight, if that's convenient.'

'Um, yes, see you at eight.'

Jade hurried to Betsy's, her curiosity now directed towards what Rick was up to and what she should wear.

When she arrived, Fi wasn't at their usual table. 'Just a tea, please,' she called to Betsy. 'I'm waiting for someone.'

'Your friend's already here,' Betsy remarked. 'Back corner table.'

Is everyone behaving strangely today, or is it me? Jade peered and waved. Fi waved back, but her heart clearly wasn't in it.

'OK, what's up?' Jade asked, almost before she'd sat down.

'Can you move a bit closer?' asked Fi.

Jade obediently shuffled her chair round. 'That do?'

Instead of answering, Fi took a plastic wrapper and a pair of tweezers from her bag. Using the tweezers and her knuckles, she extracted a piece of paper and unfolded it. Jade's heart sank when she saw the stencilled letters. 'Read that.'

Jade skimmed it, feeling herself growing angrier with every line. 'For heaven's sake,' she muttered. 'What is wrong with people?'

'What do I do?' said Fi.

As if I have any idea, thought Jade. Besides, she was fairly sure that whatever she suggested, Fi would do something else. 'What do you want to do?'

Fi folded the letter away into its envelope, then her bag, before speaking. She seemed wholly consumed by the task. 'Part of me wants to hand this to the police and let them deal with it.'

Good, good…

'But…'

Oh no, here it comes.

'Part of me wants to go along with it so that they're caught in the act.' She glanced around, then leaned closer. 'They may not be the murderer, but they know an awful lot about what's going on.'

'They seem t—'

'Here are your drinks,' said Betsy, and they both jumped as if they had been caught smoking behind the portakabin at school. 'Everything all right?'

'Yes, fine,' said Fi, in the bright tone of someone who would die rather than admit they had a problem.

'One tea and one... You did say cappuccino, didn't you?'

'I did,' said Fi.

'Good. Thought I might have made a mistake.' Betsy put the drinks down and bustled off.

Fi stared at her cappuccino, which had a cocoa heart on top, then picked up her spoon and stirred it away. 'So...'

'Has that just been delivered?'

'Zach brought it with the rest of the post, but clearly it didn't come in the mail. I should have asked him whether it was with the other letters or on its own, but I didn't think of it. I was too busy trying not to freak out.'

'I bet. And the chances of anyone noticing someone crossing *Coralie*'s gangplank is practically zero.'

'Which the person is banking on,' said Fi. 'Anyway—'

Someone cleared their throat nearby. Jade looked up and saw Sergeant Blake. 'Hello,' she said. She just stopped herself from adding something sarcastic. *Let people think he's passing the time of day. Anything else could harm Fi.* 'Pull up a chair, why don't you.'

Sergeant Blake did as he was told and sat on the opposite side of the table. 'Sorry to intrude,' he said. 'I hope you aren't having a business meeting.'

'Just a catch-up,' said Fi.

'That's good.' He shuffled his chair a bit closer and leaned in. 'Ms Booker, could you kindly tell me where you were between the hours of nine am and five pm on the day of the – the matter we discussed previously?'

Bless him, thought Jade, *he's really trying.*

Fi managed a smile. 'That's an easy one. I was at home with my son Dylan when Nerys, one of my employees, arrived at nine to open up. Zach, another employee, came at five to ten and I drove him to a college open day. In the morning I went round the stalls with him, we had lunch together, and in the afternoon I was either visiting more stalls with him or catching up on my emails in the coffee area. The open day finished at three, then I drove him to his house and had a chat with his mum about learning opportunities. I left there at five fifteen.'

'So all accounted for,' said Sergeant Blake. 'Your employees will confirm this?'

'Yes. Plus various college employees, and his mum.'

'Great, that's all I wanted.' He stood up and his chair screeched in protest. 'Carry on.'

'Do you know what this means?' murmured Jade, as soon as he had left the shop. 'They've narrowed down Bianca's time of death and you're off the hook.' Fi raised her eyebrows. 'Sorry, I mean in the clear. Blameless. Innocent.'

'I was anyway,' said Fi, taking a long drink of her cappuccino. 'It doesn't affect the other matter. I still need to make a decision about that.'

Jade sipped her tea, regarding Fi reflectively, then set the cup down. 'What a sensible person would have done,' she said, 'is give the letter to Sergeant Blake. But you didn't.'

'I was dealing with the matter at hand,' said Fi. 'He took me by surprise.'

'OK. You could still go after him. He probably parked in a car park or a side road, so people don't see the car outside a shop and get ideas.'

'He probably did,' said Fi, not moving. 'But whoever sent that letter, I want them caught red-handed. I don't want them to be able to say "Oh, it was a joke and it meant nothing." I want them to be locked up for what they've done.' She picked up a napkin and dabbed at a wet spot on the table. When she put the napkin down again, it was crumpled into a ball.

'In that case, you know what you're going to do,'

said Jade. 'My advice won't change it.'

'I suppose not,' said Fi. 'Better get back to the shop.' She drained her cup and stood up. 'I'll pay at the counter. Thanks for your help.'

'I didn't—' But Fi was already heading off.

***

Jade spent most of the afternoon worrying. She scarcely noticed Netta buzzing around the shop with armfuls of stock, humming a happy tune. In the grand scheme of things, it was nothing. *Let her have her fun.*

She barely listened when Netta told her proudly at the end of the day that the shop had achieved an average basket value of forty-five pounds. 'I kept a record,' she said, displaying a paper bag with columns of figures written neatly on it. 'You can check if you like.'

'That's fine,' said Jade. 'Congratulations.' The word seemed heavy in her mouth.

'So I can keep doing it?'

'Yes, why not.'

'Brilliant!' Netta ran over and hugged her. 'I'll put more stock out for tomorrow, then all that's left is cashing up.'

When Netta finally bounced out of the shop, Jade locked up, took herself upstairs, made a strong cup of tea, and sat on the sofa to think. An hour later, during which she had made no progress, she made a cheese sandwich, got into her pyjamas, and switched on the TV.

Thoughts chased each other round her brain. *I could text Fi and explain why it's a bad idea, but what if the police are monitoring her phone? So I can't ring her, either. Not unless we agree a code. Which the police could probably crack.*

Can the police come after you for failing to report a crime? I doubt it, but if Inspector Acaster gets involved, who knows what she'll dig out of the rule book... Jade shivered. She and Nina Acaster had parted on good terms, but she suspected it wouldn't take much to put their relationship back on an adversarial footing. She sighed and got up to make another cup of tea. When she returned to the sofa, a presenter was explaining how a CCTV camera worked.

Hmm. Is there— Could Hugo help somehow? He knows all about tech. Maybe he could rig up cameras to catch the blackmailer. That way...

'Yes!' she cried, punching the air, and popped downstairs to the shop for her notebook. Opening it to a fresh page, she flopped on the sofa and began scribbling notes and ideas. It wouldn't do to look online herself, of course. As she was a friend of Fi's, the police might be monitoring her online presence too. Or was that illegal? It ought to be, especially if Fi was in the clear. She winced at the memory of telling

Fi that she was off the hook, then carried on scribbling.

'What now,' she muttered when the doorbell rang. *No one ever calls at this time, except— Oh no.*

The bell rang again. For a moment, Jade thought of texting Rick and telling him she had a sore throat or a twisted ankle, but the guilt was too much for her. Instead, she pulled her dressing gown closely round her and opened the window. 'I'm nearly ready!' she shouted. 'Give me five minutes.'

'Sure you haven't forgotten?' said Rick, cheerily.

'Course not,' said Jade. 'Highlight of my week, this is.' She could hear him laughing as she shut the window and rushed to her bedroom.

Ten minutes later, having put on a tightish, shortish skirt and a black top which she hoped was suitably sophisticated for a wine bar, teamed with three-inch heels and dangly earrings, plus lipstick and mascara, Jade wobbled downstairs.

'You look nice,' said Rick, smiling at her.

'So do you.' He had brushed his hair and changed his usual band T-shirt and faded jeans for a pair of beige chinos and a moss-green shirt. She'd never noticed before that his eyes were green.

He looked at her feet. 'Sure you can walk in those?'

'Wouldn't wear them if I couldn't,' said Jade. 'Come on, let's hit the town.'

She was regretting the heels before they had gone twenty steps. She wasn't sure what had happened to her feet since the last time she had worn heels, but one shoe was too tight and one too loose, so that she had to clench her toes to keep it on. Plus it was warm, and she was convinced her mascara was already running. Rick made a couple of remarks, but Jade was too busy managing her footwear to say more than 'Uh-huh.'

Finally, they reached Ritzy's. Jade hoisted herself gratefully onto a barstool, which creaked. She leaned over and surveyed it. 'I'm not sure these are designed for normal-size people.'

'You're right,' said Rick. 'Look, there's a sofa free.'

They claimed it and Jade sank gratefully down, then realised her skirt had shot up to mid-thigh level. She grabbed a cushion and put it on her lap. 'You can tell I don't go to wine bars often,' she said.

'Don't be silly,' said Rick. 'Red, white, or pink?'

'Red, please,' said Jade.

When her drink arrived, in an enormous glass which made her medium measure look tiny, she sipped carefully. It was lovely, but she could actually feel it going to her head. *A cheese sandwich is no match for this*, she thought, and put down her glass. 'So, what are you working on at the moment?' she asked.

Rick launched into a description of his latest project, a set of woodcarvings he was making from fallen branches. As he talked, Jade kept a smile on her face and nodded every so often, until she registered that Rick had stopped talking and was gazing at her. 'I'm sorry,' she said. 'Things on my mind.'

'I can tell,' said Rick. 'Would it help to talk about it? I don't want to poke my nose in, but sometimes sharing helps.'

'That's very kind,' said Jade, 'but it isn't my problem.'

'Oh. That's good, I suppose.'

'Not for the person whose problem it is,' said Jade, reaching for her glass of wine.

'No, but… I wondered if you were worried about your business. I saw Netta was busy in your window earlier, writing up another offer, and I was a bit concerned.'

'Oh no, nothing to worry about there.' Jade smiled. 'Netta's chock full of ideas at the moment. My lad Hugo has been filling her head with business talk.'

'Oh dear.'

'The thing is, it's working. Much as I hate to admit it.' She went to take a sip from her glass and found that somehow it had emptied itself.

'Want another?'

Jade considered the question. On one hand, she'd only had a cheese sandwich. But she could always line her stomach with nuts, or olives, or whatever thirst-inducing snacks the wine bar had to offer. 'Why not,' she said. 'Then I can tell you about average cart value.'

'That sounds painful,' said Rick. 'Maybe I should make it a large one.'

'You don't know the half of it,' said Jade, with feeling. *One more, then I'll make my excuses*, she told herself.

'It's good to have a proper chat,' said Rick.

'As opposed to an improper chat,' Jade replied, and giggled.

'Indeed,' said Rick, smiling. 'You're a mysterious woman, Jade Fitch. I often wonder what makes you tick.'

'I'm not remotely mysterious,' Jade protested. 'Mystery just happens to me, that's all.'

'It certainly does,' said Rick, and headed for the bar.

CHAPTER 11

News of the murder was suppressed over the weekend. That was a relief, if odd. Yet despite the fact that Fi was presumably now in the clear, Marcus made no contact.

Nor did the blackmailer.

With only half her mind on her customers, Fi spent Saturday daydreaming and noting on her tablet anything that the blackmailer might have meant. She was still in a world of her own after closing, and nearly jumped out of her skin when Chloe arrived on a skateboard as she was tidying the deck.

'Hi Fi, is Dylan here? We were supposed to meet at the skatepark after he'd picked Leo Falconer's brains, but I must have missed him.'

'He went off on his bicycle ten minutes ago saying he'd be back soon,' said Fi. 'I didn't know he was meeting Leo. Is it about the exams?'

Chloe shrugged. 'Can I help with those signs and chairs?'

'Don't worry,' said Fi. 'The signs go in the wheelhouse and the chairs stay out. Feel free to come up and wait. Want anything to drink?'

'No, thanks.' Chloe took a seat and with a giggle, shook hands with Stan. 'Isn't he a lovely dog? It's nice here. Dylan's soooo lucky. I hope you don't mind me hanging out. Are you sure I can't help with anything?'

'Honestly, no.' Fi smiled, wishing Dylan were half as polite these days.

The man himself rode up as if the hounds of hell were after him, threw his bicycle on the grass and rushed over the gangplank. 'What are you doing, Chloe? You should have waited. You shouldn't be walking on your own by the river!'

Chloe stared at him, then giggled again. 'It's only Hazeby. Nothing happens here, except to *old* people. Anyway, I learned judo when I was a kid.' She flicked her hands in a unconvincing manner. 'I don't need a hero. I can look after myself.'

Dylan blushed scarlet. 'It's just… Yeah, of course you can. I hope Mum hasn't been embarrassing.'

'Your mum's lovely. Have you asked about the band?'

'What about the band?' Fi raised her eyebrows at Dylan.

'You'll say no, anyway.'

'To what?'

'Us jamming on the deck one evening when the exams are over.'

'I could stand at the pointy bit and sing *My Heart Will Go On*,' said Chloe.

Fi hadn't thought Dylan could go redder, but he managed. 'Er, what?'

'From *Titanic*.'

Dylan looked blank.

'It's a film from when I was at uni,' said Fi. 'As for jamming – yes, of course, if you tell me when. Then I can warn people and maybe get a licence if the council are picky.'

Dylan frowned. 'That's not very spon—'

'Thanks a million, Fi,' said Chloe. 'You can stay and listen, if you like.'

'No she can't,' said Dylan, scowling. 'She'll be on a hot date. Won't you, Mum?'

'Not if you don't tell me when,' said Fi, wondering if she'd ever go on any sort of date again.

'Are you going out soon, so we can have the boat to ourselves?'

'Sorry,' she said, inwardly shuddering at the thought of having to do The Talk. 'It may be Saturday night but I'm definitely in. Carla's coming over for a drink later. You two can join us, if you want.'

'You're so embarrassing, Mum.' Dylan glared at

her. 'Come on, Chloe. Let's see if there's anyone interesting hanging out at the burger place.'

***

He'd mellowed a little the following day, when they went to Gavin's parents.

Fi made the most of being looked after and eating a delicious meal she hadn't had to cook herself. It was a shame her appetite was lacking, but it went unnoticed as Annie refilled Dylan's plate yet again, to his evident delight.

Afterwards, Annie and Nigel went to doze in the garden. Dylan nudged Fi. 'Can you help?'

'With what?'

'Something in Dad's room. Nana said he had a good-luck charm when he did his GCSEs.'

'He did? I mean yes, of course.'

'Nana said he aced his exams,' said Dylan, as they climbed the stairs. 'Maybe I can channel him.'

'I'm not sure your dad aced exams,' said Fi. 'He winged things and it usually worked. It never works for me. So don't take it as a model for success, because you're half of each of us.'

She looked round a room which had only changed a little since Gavin had left home at eighteen. When they'd come to stay after their marriage, tattered posters of football teams, cars and rock groups were still stuck on the walls with Blu-Tack.

Since Gavin's death, the Bookers had redecorated,

but they'd framed the posters and hung them amongst Gavin's school photos and his university graduation photograph. There were a few children's and young adult books in the bookcase, with some toys, models and figurines. Even though the remnants of Gavin were minimal, the room, which Dylan slept in if they ever stayed over, still gave the impression that it was waiting for its owner to return.

'Which one's Dad?' asked Dylan, staring at the school pictures.

Fi peered, then pointed. 'That one and that one. He's got the same grin as you. Same eyes.'

'I'm not much like him otherwise,' said Dylan, pointing at the posters. 'Perhaps I would have been if he'd brought me up.' It sounded like an accusation.

'There's no way of telling,' said Fi. 'If you'd wanted football and cars, I wouldn't have stopped you. Turned out you like music, acting and boats. Be you.'

'Hmmph. So where's this lucky charm?'

Fi racked her brains. She glanced sideways at her son, keeping her voice as light as possible. 'Do you believe in luck?'

'Not really, but Nana does. It'll make her happy if I find the charm.'

'It was probably something she gave him. Maybe...' Fi picked up a small figure of Superman with a scroll in his hand. 'This?'

'That?' said Dylan. 'Would Dad have taken *that* to

school at sixteen?'

For the first time in days, Fi grinned. 'If he did, I bet he kept it buried in his school bag!'

Dylan took the figure from her. 'Maybe…'

Rubbing her eyes, Annie entered the room. 'You found it! I'm so glad. It connects you.' She touched the boy Fi had picked out in the year eleven school photograph. 'I know you'll be a credit to him.'

'Have you got any other physical photos, Annie?' asked Fi, mentally crossing her fingers. 'I'm sure Dylan would like to see them.'

'I've got albums. I ought to get them scanned.'

'I'll do it,' said Dylan. 'Can I take photos from when Dad was my age and from when he and Mum and me were together?'

Annie glanced at Fi, then nodded.

Dylan tossed the little Superman in the air and caught it, his eyes following the figure rather than focusing on anyone. 'Nana, what would you do if you found out Dad had lied to you?'

It hadn't been if, thought Fi. *It had been when.*

'Try to work out why,' said Annie, looking sad but also a little defiant. Fi willed herself to respond with an encouraging smile, but what Bianca had said made it hard. Gavin had broken both their hearts. Surely he wasn't alive to do it again?

***

Fi prepared to open the shop on Monday morning,

102

hoping she'd have more chance to go through Annie's photos than she had done the previous day, when Dylan had taken them to his cabin.

Dylan came to breakfast dishevelled and grey about the eyes. 'A week today it'll be English Lit,' he said gloomily, staring into his cereal as if it were an abyss full of starving sharks.

'Focus on five weeks today instead,' said Fi, hugging his shoulders. 'The exams will be over before you know it.'

'I didn't revise yesterday. I'll have to do double today. And I promised I'd scan those photos.'

'I'll dig out the best ones for when you have a break.'

'I haven't got time for breaks. I'm going to fail everything.'

'Yes you have, and no, you won't. Give me the photos and I'll get you a bacon butty at eleven.'

Dylan brightened a little. 'You're on.' He collected the photo albums and the Superman figure from his cabin. 'Will this charm help?'

'No,' said Fi. She picked it up and frowned. How had she known which of the little figures was the lucky charm? Gavin must have told her. Or was it something else? 'Dylan, what did you mean when you asked Nana what she'd do if your dad had lied to her?'

'I dunno,' said Dylan, squirming a little. 'You

know what he did. She seems to have forgiven him. Would—'

A cry of 'Post!' rang from the wheelhouse.

Fi felt herself go hot, then cold. She couldn't risk Dylan seeing a letter from the blackmailer. 'I'll go.' She rushed up the steps. 'You're early,' she said to the postman.

'Getting my round done while it's still cool,' he said. 'See ya.'

Heart hammering, Fi returned to the shop to flick through the post. There was nothing untoward.

'Mum!' called Dylan. 'Marcus is calling your mobile. I'm going to my cabin before things get slushy.'

Relief flooding in, Fi grabbed her phone, answered the call and ran up to the deck. *Finally*. If she could find the right place to stand, where no one could hear her, she'd tell him about the letter. 'Hi,' she said.

'You went out of town yesterday.'

'We went to Annie's for lunch and tea. Oh no, did I miss you?'

'You were told not to leave town during the investigation!'

'But Sergeant Blake said—'

'I know what you're trying to say,' said Marcus. 'You don't know what a certain person is saying about me giving you leeway that I wouldn't give to any other witness.'

'I'm sorry *your* life is being ruined by all this,' snapped Fi. 'I never realised that me getting away from things for a few hours would spoil *your* day.'

'Fi, I didn't mean—'

'Was there anything else, Inspector?' she said. 'No? Then I'll let you get on with your investigation. I have a new boathook to buy.'

She waited for him to apologise, but after the briefest of pauses, Marcus said, 'Please store the next one properly.'

'I can think of the perfect place for it,' she said. 'Goodbye.'

She shoved the phone in her pocket with a growl and flicked through the mail again. Surely, if the blackmail was real, there'd be another letter by now. Maybe it was just as well she hadn't told Marcus. Perhaps someone had seen Bianca's body taken from the river, and they wanted to make her miserable for some bizarre reason of their own. But what was *the stuff you've never told anyone*? The list of things Fi had never told anyone was quite long, but this implied something specific.

Then there was the man she'd seen. If it was Gavin, surely he'd either greet her or keep hidden until the right moment. If it wasn't, why risk being seen at all?

Nothing added up, and she had to find out why so that she'd have something concrete to help Marcus.

Because, irritating as Marcus was being just now, Fi suddenly knew she wasn't ready to let him go. Not for anyone. Not even a long-dead husband.

CHAPTER 12

Netta grinned as she set a steaming mug in front of Jade. 'Good weekend, was it?'

'Fine, thanks. You?'

'Yeah. I went for brunch on Sunday, then watched part of an online course I'm doing.'

'Oh, right. What's it for?'

'It's called *Bitesize Business Bonus*. Each video's three minutes or less, and the host is this woman who wears a headband with bouncy cats on.'

'Deelyboppers.'

'No, she's called Anthea. She's really good at explaining things, but I keep getting distracted by the cats.'

'Ah.' Jade thought about asking what Netta had learned, then decided she didn't want to know, much less have an argument over implementing it.

'So what did you get up to?' said Netta.

'Just a quiet weekend,' said Jade. 'Life admin. Ooh, customer.'

Netta immediately stepped forward, ready to upsell based on whatever the hapless person had in their hands. *At least she's easy to distract.*

Jade was still getting over the weekend. She had woken on Sunday feeling uncomfortable and stiff, as if she was in a strange place. *I didn't, did I?*

Without opening her eyes, she listened. She couldn't hear anything unusual, like the sound of someone else breathing. *Phew.* Next, she reached beneath the covers and cautiously explored what she was wearing. It was the outfit of the night before, and her bra was still on. *OK.* She opened one eye, and could have shouted for joy when she realised she was lying on her own sofa, under her own duvet.

Oh, the relief. She let out a happy sigh. *Time for a celebratory cup of tea.* But as she swung her legs down, her foot caught something hard. A mug had been upended and water was spreading over the rug.

'Damn!' Jade jumped up and got a cloth, and as she did she saw her high-heeled shoes, placed neatly by the door.

I'm never that organised. I certainly wouldn't remember to get myself some water after a night out. I'd just collapse on the bed. An awful possibility struck her. *Oh no...*

She tiptoed to to the bedroom door, gently pushed

down the handle and peeped round it.

The room was empty.

I'm never drinking again. I can't cope with this kind of tension. Then she reflected. *The next time I go for a drink, I'll make sure I have a proper meal first. Flaming cheese sandwich. Flaming ginormous wine glasses.* Muttering to herself, she stomped to the kettle and switched it on.

As it was psyching itself up to boil, her phone buzzed.

Jade glared at it, then reflected that at least she hadn't managed to lose it. However, having her phone meant that people she didn't necessarily want to speak to could contact her.

I should look at that, she thought, *in case it's Fi.*

I'll make tea first.

She leaned on the worktop and stared at the kettle. Once it had boiled, she gave the tea a good five minutes to brew. *If ever I need the caffeine, it's now.*

Finally, brew in hand, she sat on the sofa and picked up her phone.

Of course it wasn't Fi. *Good morning :-) Hope you're feeling all right. I enjoyed last night and hope you did too. Speak soon, Rick*

'I enjoyed last night' – what does that mean? I didn't, did I? Jade sipped her tea, which a builder might have found a little strong, and pondered what to reply. If anything.

She made a few false starts, but eventually typed: *I'm fine, thanks, though I don't remember much after the second glass of wine*, and pressed *Send*. There. That would convey that whatever had happened, she wasn't responsible.

But what had happened? She had a vague memory of talking about Netta's plans for world domination before Rick had said 'Let's not talk about work all night.'

What did I talk about? I didn't talk about Fi, did I?

Her phone buzzed again. *Don't worry, you were very well-behaved. Although I did have to rescue your shoes from a bin.*

Jade felt a strong urge to wail at the universe, but as Rick was next door she contented herself with a silent scream into a cushion. *Sorry*, she typed afterwards.

It was fun. Maybe we should go back.

Jade considered this. Hopefully, that meant she hadn't disgraced herself and been banned from Ritzy's. *I'll be super busy next week*, she typed, and pressed *Send* before she could second-guess herself.

Thought you might say that :-)

Jade threw the phone down and growled.

And now, on Monday morning, she was still in no mood to face a queue of customers.

'Going well, isn't it?' said Netta. 'That new offer is pulling people in.'

'Um, yes,' said Jade. Then she noticed a man fidgeting halfway down the queue. He looked familiar, but she couldn't place him. And he didn't seem to have anything to buy.

He caught her eye, then advanced to the counter and held out his hand. 'Jade, good to see you again. I was in town and thought I'd pop in. I'm organising another event at Spetisham Hall in October and I wanted to book you.'

Of course! Simon, the events organiser. 'I'll have to check my diary,' she said. 'October's busy for us, for obvious reasons. But if you let me have the dates, I'm sure we can sort something out.'

'Great.' He smiled, but his eyes were roaming over the shop. 'Can you give me your mobile number? Then I can text them to you.'

'I gave you my number before the festival,' said Jade.

'Oh yes, so you did. Sorry. Monday-morning blues. Right, I'll send those to you and let you get on.' He hurried out of the shop.

Hmm. The Simon she had met at Spetisham Hall had been professionalism itself. This one was going through the motions. *He must be really upset about Bianca, and soldiering on to try and push through it.*

'Excuse me?' called the customer second in line.

Netta was busy serving. 'How can I help?' asked Jade.

111

'Do you have any more four-leaf clover charms? I want to buy one for each of my daughters, and you only have one left.'

'Good idea,' said the man behind her. 'Young women need to watch out at the moment. Stay indoors, or travel in groups.'

'*They* shouldn't have to stay indoors,' said the woman Netta was serving, turning and glaring at him. 'Murderers shouldn't murder.'

'I know that, but there's no harm in being careful while the police find the murderer.'

'*If* they find the murderer,' said Clover Woman. 'I haven't seen any police anywhere.'

'Me neither,' said the man. 'They should be knocking on the door of every boat and barge on the river. They know the murderer used a boathook. What's keeping them?'

An angry buzz of chatter rose. Jade clapped her hands. 'Just because the murderer used a boathook, that doesn't mean they live on a boat.' *Oh, Fi.*

'It doesn't mean they didn't,' said the woman being served. 'Plus, with a boat, they could do the deed, lift the anchor and sail away scot-free.'

'I'm sure the police have it in hand,' said Jade. 'And I'm sure they've been monitoring the movement of boats, among other things.' She resolved to write down that point in her notebook later, though.

'Flaming floating hippies,' said the man.

'Wandering around in tie-dye and dreadlocks, making the town look untidy.'

If you're against alternative culture, thought Jade, *what are you doing in my shop?*

'Hazeby doesn't feel safe any more,' said Clover Woman. 'It's a disgrace that we have to buy charms for ourselves and our loved ones. Honestly, we're grasping at straws.'

'You don't have to buy charms,' said Jade. 'What you should do is be careful, at least for now. *Everyone* should be careful, not just young women. You don't know what's in this person's mind.'

'We don't,' said the man. 'And it could be a whole gang of them. I see teenagers hanging around on the riverbank all the time, and they're probably up to no good.'

'Never mind the teenagers,' said the woman at the head of the queue. 'I heard there's a man lurking in the bushes by the river. If it's anyone, it's him.' This stirred up the crowd to new heights.

Jade glanced at Netta, whose expression was a mixture of confusion and frustration. 'Right, everyone!' she shouted. The customers faced her. 'Instead of flinging accusations around, let's concentrate on what we can do. Stay safe, and make sure your friends and family do, too. That'll be more effective than any number of good-luck charms. But if you do want one, I've decided to make them half price.'

Netta stared at her, slack-jawed. 'But—'

'I don't care if it's good business sense or not, Netta. Hopefully, the charms will remind people to watch out and take care. And of course, if you see anything at all odd, make sure you report it.'

There were various nods and mumbles. The woman at the head of the queue scratched her ear. 'Um, could I go and get a charm?'

'I'll bring some to the counter,' said Jade. 'Then I'll check what we have in the stockroom. Netta, if you wouldn't mind serving.'

Netta jumped as if Jade had startled her into life. 'Of course not,' she said, and began entering purchases.

Jade unhooked a selection of charms, leaving one of each in place on the wall. *At least they don't know it's Fi's boathook. Yet.* She resolved to suggest a meet-up with Fi as soon as she had a free moment. *I must warn her.* And as she brought the charms to the counter, where hands reached for them immediately, she wished firstly that the darn things worked, and secondly, that Fi could be persuaded to wear one.

CHAPTER 13

'Did you know?' said an elegant customer in her fifties with well-cut silver hair and blue eyes glinting behind designer glasses. 'They pulled someone out of the water last Friday. A teenage girl. Held under.' Her gaze flicked towards Zach for a second as he came down to collect more stock for the deck. It seemed as if she was the four hundredth customer who'd said something similar, and it was only mid-morning.

'That's not what I heard,' said another customer with a pile of books. 'An old lady was clobbered with a boat fender.'

'Boathook,' declared a young woman with a handful of gifts for small children. 'That's what it was. It was someone in her thirties. And she wasn't hit, she fell. Probably she was trying to get it and they found her floating.'

'That's a myth,' said the one who thought it had

115

been a teenager. 'Bodies don't float straight away. They don't appear for weeks. So maybe that's how long she's been there.'

'That'll be eighteen ninety-eight, please,' said Fi firmly. 'Card or cash?' She felt some level of relief that the news was out, even if it had been mangled by gossip within a few hours. She just wished Marcus had warned her when he'd phoned. On the other hand, he'd started on the wrong foot and she hadn't given him the chance to move onto the right one. Maybe he'd intended to tell her, but hadn't had the chance. *He could have rung back*, she thought grumpily. *But I could have, too.*

'Card,' said the customer. 'Thanks. Any of the boat community missing?'

'I don't believe so,' said Fi. 'Maybe we should all wait until the police release more information before speculating. They need to be able to investigate.'

'Of course,' said the older woman. 'You're an expert.' She smiled brightly and put a pile of classic mysteries on the counter. *Death on the Nile* was on top, *Dead Water* next. 'You and that Ms Fitch. She's selling lucky charms like they're going out of fashion.'

'Good for Jade,' said Fi, suppressing a smirk. She couldn't compete on the superstitious customer front and there was no point trying.

Nerys came down the steps and paused to greet the

woman with the toys, then walked up to Fi. 'Have you—'

'Heard that a body was taken from the river on Friday? Yes,' said Fi. 'Can you take over for a bit? I promised Dylan I'd get him a bacon sandwich from Betsy's and I have things to go through in private.'

'Sure,' said Nerys. 'I wonder if it's a local. I haven't heard anything. Or maybe it's a tourist. They're forever falling in.'

Fi rolled her eyes. 'If tourists were forever falling in, they'd put a fence up.' She had a brief moment of hope that perhaps that was what had happened. Then she realised that if it was that simple, the police wouldn't have wanted to know her whereabouts on Friday after she'd explained she might have a reason to want Bianca dead.

It was nice to get away from the boat for a while, but she didn't feel like walking by the river. She took Stan towards the park, watching the tourists mill about in their bright clothes. The ghost tour was underway, and Kevin was holding forth outside a half-timbered Tudor building that had been the scene of a mysterious death in 1575. His audience appeared to be four enthusiasts and three cynics, plus a toddler with an ice cream at a dangerous angle.

'And when she lifted the lid…' said Kevin. The ice cream slipped out of the cornet and onto the sandalled foot of one of the cynics. Both cynic and toddler shrieked, and Fi had never seen Kevin look so proud of himself. Normally, she'd have laughed, but right now it was impossible not to notice a number of police officers with clipboards, stopping people to ask questions.

Sergeant Blake came over to greet her. 'Hello, Ms Booker.'

'So the news is out at last.'

'We wanted it quiet while we did a bit of background digging.'

'I take it the body was Bianca.'

'Yes,' he said. 'We're still not releasing the name. So far, no one's reported her missing, either. That suggests a few things, and we need to follow them up without spooking anyone.'

'Can you say how she died? I've heard every rumour under the sun this morning.'

Sergeant Blake glanced round to make sure no one was in earshot and leaned in. 'I'm only telling you cos you know a bit and the boss trusts you. It looks like she was struck with the blunt end of the boathook, fell, and drowned while unconscious. At a guess, they threw the boathook in after her, thinking it – and maybe she – would float off, or that she and the boathook would sink and get pulled along by the current. The initial blow could have been an accident, but not going for help…' He pulled a face. 'Have you remembered anything else useful about your

118

encounter with her?'

Fi shook her head. 'I told you everything we both said. I don't know what she said to Simon. I've given you the reference number for the Italian police case into Gavin's presumed death.' Should she mention the blackmail? No: it had to be a hoax. No one would send a blackmailing letter to arrive on Friday and not follow it up by Monday. If she'd had a sensible conversation with Marcus earlier, she'd have told him about it so that he could reassure her, but Sergeant Blake had enough on his plate.

'Any strange men lurking by the river?'

'Rrrerrfff,' said Stan, pulling on the lead. *Traitor.*

'He took a dislike to someone last…' Fi thought. 'Last Wednesday. I was going to give him a piece of my mind but he ran off.'

The sergeant extracted his notebook. 'Age? Appearance?'

'Late forties, average to tall in height, a little overweight, perhaps – thick set, anyway – greying at the temples, tanned, a bit stubbly.'

'Down and out?'

'I didn't get that impression.'

'Familiar?'

'Not from town.' Fi had compared that brief sighting with her memory of a photograph seen at dusk and with Nigel, Gavin's father, in photographs at a similar age. She couldn't swear to anything. But not to put it forward as a possibility was something else. 'He looked similar to the photograph Bianca showed me. I couldn't say they were the same under oath: I didn't get a proper look at either. Have you got the photographs?'

'Unless you count mushy bits of card which could be anything, not so far.' Sergeant Blake made a final squiggle in his notebook. 'Thanks, Ms Booker.' He strode away.

'Rrrerrfff,' said Stan, pulling again.

'What is it?' said Fi, letting him lead her. In the churchyard, a small group of women were attaching flowers to the lych gate. Beyond them, people milled round the ancient tombstones, reading the inscriptions. Through the open church door she could make out pale walls and light coming through stained glass. 'Dogs aren't welcome in graveyards. Besides, I've bacon butties to buy, and maybe a butty without bread for you... What do you think? Sausages?'

'Rrrerrfff!' Stan headed for Betsy's at a trot.

A few minutes later, they walked back to the boat with a bag of butties and pastries and a foil container of sausages. There was no need to hurry. Nothing would get cold, and the police seemed to be in control of the Bianca situation. Fi felt herself relax. She messaged Jade to ask her round for the evening and help repel teenagers intent on who knew what, but decided to wait till later before messaging Marcus and making peace. He rarely replied when he was on duty, so there was little point. Maybe he'd reach out first.

But at seven, when she and Jade returned from walking Stan and catching up, Fi was hailed by the owner of a narrowboat moored a few metres away. Angie and her partner lived on board, slowly working their way around the waterways, stopping for months at a time and periodically leaving to visit relations by train. Fi hadn't seen either of them for a few days.

'Hi,' she said. 'Hope you've had a good trip.'

'Lovely, thanks,' said Angie. 'Our daughter was getting married. But it seems there's been a tragedy downriver, which has dampened things a bit.'

'Yes, it's awful.' Fi's heart sank a little, wondering what she'd be asked next.

'The police are on it, though.' Angie chuckled. 'They were on the boat asking a million questions within ten minutes of us getting back. Not that we could tell them anything, of course. Anyway, I was about to come round. The postman delivered this to the wrong boat.' She handed over a plastic envelope with a printed label.

Fi's mood nose-dived.

'Is everything all right?' said Angie.

'Oh, er, yes. Annoying client.'

'We'd best get to *Coralie*,' said Jade. 'The takeaway's due any minute.'

'Congratulations on the wedding.' Fi forced herself

to sound bright and breezy.

'Thanks! Come for cake and look at the photos later in the week!'

'Definitely.' Fi and Jade scurried to *Coralie*, checked Dylan was definitely out, then sat down with tweezers to open the envelope.

The police are on to you. That policeman boyfriend of yours hasn't been around at all, has he? Which makes you top suspect. All the town knows it's a boathook, so it's only a matter of time before they find out whose. I can help . . . or I can hinder. Expect instructions on Tuesday. Don't tell the police, or things will get even worse. Don't think I'm not watching you.

Fi sat back and Jade narrowed her eyes. 'You're suspiciously cheerful.'

'They don't know I have an alibi,' said Fi. 'That means they don't know everything. They're chancing their arm. They're amateurs.'

'How do you know how expert blackmailers behave?' asked Jade, waving a hand towards the bookshop. 'Novels? TV dramas? You need to tell Marcus.'

'Not yet.'

Jade reached out to feel Fi's forehead. 'That's the sort of hare-brained thing I'd say. There's something very wrong when I'm the sensible one.'

'I'll go along with them,' said Fi, ignoring her. 'I

want to know who they are and what they think they know. I want to know if it's the man I saw. If it's Gavin, so help me—'

'Shh,' said Jade. 'Walls – boats have ears. One step at a time. Oh flip, there's me being sensible again. Never mind. What did Gavin look like?'

Fi collected an album from Dylan's cabin. It fell open at the place where he'd left a marker: their wedding photograph. She felt as if she were looking at strangers.

'OK,' said Jade. 'I recognise his dad from Christmas. I guess that in this photo he was maybe ten years older than Gavin would be now?'

'About that. They're quite similar. More than Dylan and Gavin.'

'And the man in the photo and the bushes?'

'It's so hard to say,' said Fi. 'He was more tanned, greyer, plumper. I only had seconds, and—'

'You'd been primed to see what Bianca wanted you to see. Mmm.' Jade poured them each a glass of wine and handed over Fi's phone. 'Ring Marcus.'

'If I appear to comply with the blackmailers, they'll reveal themselves. Then I'll have something to tell him. It's me they want to torment and ruin. I'll do it alone if necessary.'

'Forget that,' said Jade. 'We're a team, and I won't let them get you. Now, what's the plan? And I don't suppose you want a lucky charm, do you?'

CHAPTER 19

Jade moved around the shop, adjusting a book here and a CD there, wishing they were properly busy.

She had been twitchy ever since meeting Fi the day before, when what she now thought of as *the letter* had arrived.

'I still think it's a terrible idea,' she had said.

'Going along with the blackmailer?' said Fi. 'It would be, if I didn't have a plan.'

'Do you have a plan?'

'Not yet.' Fi tapped the side of her head. 'I'm working on it.'

Jade wasn't sure how she felt about this new, reckless Fi. *I'm not used to being the sensible half.* In her head, she said sorry to Fi for all the times when she must have worried her sick with various daft schemes. *Maybe I'm just getting old and cautious. I can see why Fi's angry, of course I can, but surely there's another way to tackle it?*

'If you do go ahead,' she found herself saying, 'maybe Hugo can advise us on surveillance.'

Fi brightened. 'Hidden cameras? That's a good idea. Can you ask him and let me know?'

'I'm not asking him that using my own phone!' said Jade. 'The police could be monitoring us both. Which reminds me, we ought to have some sort of code.'

'I'm not sure the police are allowed to do that,' said Fi. 'It's probably disproportionate.'

'I'm taking no chances.' Jade searched her brain for a phrase she might remember. 'OK. If you do go along with the blackmailer, text me something like...'

'I bought that book on investments I was telling you about?' Fi suggested.

'That'll do. Yes, good, because then you could ask if I want to read it, meaning will I help. And if you decide to tell the police and stay out of it, you can tell me you didn't buy the book.' Jade felt it was important to give Fi a definite option for not embroiling herself in more trouble.

'OK, whatever,' said Fi. 'I really don't think we're being monitored. Anyway, I can't make a decision until the blackmailer sends more information. Which will be tomorrow.'

'Yes.' Jade studied Fi. Her eyes were bright and there was a no-nonsense air about her. 'Fi...'

'Yes?'

'Please don't get involved in something dangerous because you can't stand doing nothing. The blackmailer's playing you.'

'If so, they're doing a good job. I'm itching to get my hands on them.' Fi's hands clenched into fists.

'For all you know, they're professionals. Please be careful.'

'I will. And yes, I'd like your help. If you're willing.'

'Of course.'

Fi raised an eyebrow. 'Sure?'

'Yep. Sure.' Jade hoped she sounded surer than she felt.

And now it was Tuesday, when another communication would come from the blackmailer. Jade felt as if she had been on standby since the moment she woke.

Her twitchiness hadn't been helped by running into Rick first thing, in the queue at Betsy's.

'Hello there,' said a familiar voice.

Jade composed her expression before turning. 'Oh, hello. I didn't know you came in here.'

'I don't often,' said Rick, patting his middle. 'Bad for the waistline. But some days just require bacon.'

'Oh,' said Jade.

She was about to turn back when Rick said, 'Are you still busy this week?'

'It is a bit fraught, yes,' said Jade. 'Probably late finishes. Planning the next quarter, that sort of thing.'

Rick smiled. 'From what you said the other day, I got the impression that young Netta was more of a planner than you.'

'I wouldn't say that,' said Jade, wondering what on earth she *had* said. 'I just tend to keep it in my head more.'

Rick grinned. 'Well, it seems to be working.'

'Next!' called the young man behind the counter.

Jade stepped up and placed her order. She had been intending to get a bacon sandwich herself, but the thought of making small talk with Rick while they both waited for their food made her curl up inside. As soon as she was served, she said goodbye and hurried out.

When she was outside, her pace slowed. *He didn't follow me, did he?*

Come off it, said the inner voice that still plagued her from time to time, though it spoke less often than it had previously. *Given that you can't even remember what you did or said at the wine bar, he was probably as freaked out to see you as you were to see him.*

Thanks a bunch, thought Jade, and absentmindedly sipped her coffee. 'Ow!' It was still far too hot to drink.

And her problems didn't end there. She made herself toast to replace the bacon sandwich – not that it could – and was about to take a bite when she heard Netta letting herself into the shop. *I wasn't that long, was I?* But when she checked the time, it was eight fifteen. Fighting the urge to growl, mostly in case Netta or Rick heard, she bolted her toast and took the coffee downstairs.

'Morning,' said Netta, hanging up her bag and shaking out her long brown hair. 'Lovely day, isn't it?'

'You're early.'

'I woke up early. It must have been the sunshine. A new day, full of opportunities.'

'Mmm.' Jade took the lid off her coffee and blew on it. As she drank, she watched Netta over the rim of the cup.

'I've had a bit of an idea,' said Netta.

'Have you.'

'Yes. It was partly that Bitesize course, and partly something Hugo said.'

'You don't want to believe everything Hugo says.'

Netta's eyes widened. 'Why not? He runs a successful business.'

'In a completely different field.'

Netta held up a finger. 'Or is it?'

'Yes, it flaming well is,' said Jade. 'This is a crystal and magic shop, and Hugo's business is – is – entirely different.'

'It's to do with technology, isn't it? And computers. We could do that.'

'Excuse me?' Jade peered into her coffee, wondering whether she'd been drugged.

'We could have an e-store.'

Jade took a gulp of the coffee. If there was something funny about it, maybe drinking more would bring her out on the other side. 'An e-store?'

'Yeah. Everyone's got a website, but we could do e-commerce too.'

'But – but how?' Jade's head was spinning, and on balance, she thought it was due to Netta rather than the coffee.

'You already have a brand – Crystal Dreams – and shop colours. We just need an online storefront. Then we could list popular items that are easy to pack and post and sell them all over the world, potentially.' Netta leaned on the counter and cupped her chin in her hands. 'We could have gift boxes, and purple tissue, and Crystal Dreams stickers…'

Oh my.

'Hugo thinks it's a great idea.'

'Does he now,' Jade said, grimly.

'Yes. He thinks there's a great opportunity for quirky niche businesses to have an online presence.'

'I don't even know where to start with that sentence,' said Jade. 'Actually, yes I do.' She pulled out her phone and typed a message. *Please don't lead Netta down the garden path. Love Mum.* She pressed *Send.* Hopefully, it would wake Hugo. Despite his protestations of early meetings and whatnot, he'd always been a terrible slugabed.

A reply came thirty seconds later. *Good morning, Mummy. I can assure you that my intentions regarding Netta are entirely honourable.*

Jade sighed. *I'm sure they are, and I don't mind who you go out with. But please leave my business alone.*

So you don't mind if I go out with Netta?

Jade rolled her eyes. *Of course not. Does she want to go out with you?*

Very funny. Got to go, early tutorial.

'Ha!' Jade put down her phone.

'So does that mean I can go ahead?' said Netta.

'What? No! Um . . . I don't know.' Jade racked her brains for a way to let Netta down gently. 'I need a business case.'

Netta goggled at her. 'A business case?'

'Yes. What you're proposing is practically a whole new business. It's certainly a new arm of the business that we have. I mean, how much does a storefront cost? Do we need a licence? How much stock would we need, and could we store it here? How much will postage be? What if it takes off?'

'Don't you want it to take off?' Netta asked, looking hurt.

'I don't know how much work it will be, or whether it's worth doing. Which is why I'd like to see a business case.'

'All right.' Netta set her jaw, then went to her bag and took out a purple notebook with a unicorn on it. Tucked into the band was a purple pen with a fluffy top. 'I'll work on it when the shop's quiet.'

'Fine. But the customers come first.'

Netta drew herself up. 'Of course.'

Jade secretly hoped a wave of customers would sweep Netta's business case under the carpet, where it could be quietly forgotten. But it was unusually quiet, even for a Tuesday, and it wasn't as if there was anything else for Netta to do. Jade found herself wondering whether an online store might be a good idea, then shook herself and went out for Danish pastries. She crossed the road then went the long way round to avoid going past Rick's shop.

The day wore on. Jade ordered more silver charms, since they were down to the last few, and Netta broke off from frowning at her notebook to suggest more items they should stock up on.

'What's that?' asked Jade, motioning at four arrows like points of the compass, with various things scribbled next to them.

'It's a SWOT analysis.'

'Right. And what does it do?'

'It stands for strengths, weaknesses, opportunities, and threats.' Netta's purple pen indicated each arrow in turn. 'It's used for—'

Jade's phone buzzed. 'Hang on a minute,' she said, reaching for it. Then she froze. Who would it be? Hopefully it was Hugo, trying to get the last word. Or maybe Rick, teasing her gently about their rendezvous the week before. Or… She wouldn't even mind if it was Marcus Falconer, letting her know that everything was sorted or asking an easy question. But there was one person she definitely didn't want it to be.

'Are you going to read it or not?' said Netta, grinning.

'Yeah,' Jade replied. 'Fancy a brew? That looks like thirsty work.'

'Don't mind if I do.'

'OK.' Jade grabbed her phone and hurried into the back room. She switched the kettle on, then took mugs from the cupboard and dropped in two teabags. She fetched the milk from the fridge. She found a teaspoon.

Only then did she check her phone.

The message was from Fi, but she couldn't see what it said without opening it.

Jade took a deep breath and touched the little white box with her thumb.

Hi, just to let you know I decided to buy that book on investments. I've received some interesting new information. Would you like to read it too?

Jade put down her phone. The kettle was rising to its grand finale and she felt as if her own brain was bubbling. *No*, she thought. *No, I wouldn't. And I wish you wouldn't, Fi. But I said I'd help, and I will.*

CHAPTER 15

Fi woke early but energised on Tuesday morning.

Perhaps you should spend more time taking risks and less time being sensible, she thought as she drank a pre-run coffee. *Look what happened when you gave up a comfy corporate job and started the Book Barge.*

You planned the Book Barge during your lunch breaks and quiet evenings for years, whispered another thought. *And you weren't dealing with criminals – even possibly amateur ones. Ring Marcus. What would you say if Jade was doing this?*

Telling both thoughts to pipe down, Fi called Stan and made her way through the barge. The previous evening, she had gone to bed leaving Dylan sprawled on the sofa with a notebook and the set novels for his exam. They were still strewn everywhere.

She resolved to get Dylan out of bed when she returned and make him tidy up, then realised the books were new ones from her shelves. Some were open face-down on the sofa. How dare Dylan risk damaging her stock? She picked up *Epic Bike Rides Of The World,* which was sitting on two books about camping off the beaten track and sustainable travelling through Europe. Never mind getting Dylan out of bed on her return: she should wake him now.

But she needed the run to clear her mind for what lay ahead, not for an argument, and she had to keep her wits about her. If the man reappeared…

Even the newly liberated risk-taking part of her brain didn't want to run along the river while it was nearly deserted. With Stan at her heels, she ran into town. She passed the minimart as it opened its shutters, paperboys and papergirls loading their bags at the newsagent, and other shops and cafés as they came to life. She saw nothing unusual, and when she returned to the boat the books had been put away and Dylan was making breakfast.

'Sorry about the mess, Mum,' he said. 'I needed something to, um, make Venice come alive. You know, Merchant Of. Shakespeare. I reckon it would be improved with bikes and tents. I might do a rewrite as a project sometime.'

'Oh.'

'I didn't damage anything, promise,' said Dylan. 'And I've given everything a dust. Go and have a shower. I'll make you more coffee.' It was unnerving how much more annoying Dylan was when he was being nice, but it seemed pointless to argue.

Agonisingly, the post didn't arrive until well into the morning. Fi told Dylan to take a break from revising and lend a hand on deck, then shut herself up with the letter.

Leave a supermarket bag with £5000 in cash in the bin by the rowing club by twelve noon. Don't hang around. Don't even think about telling the police. If there's no funny business, I'll be in touch for one final instalment. Be warned – it'll be larger.

'I'm popping to town,' she told Zach. 'I'll take Stan for another walk, too.' She tried to ignore the disappointment on his face. She'd been promising him that they'd discuss the website for days.

The bank had changed its layout and now only employed two cashiers, on the grounds that everyone did their banking online these days. Presumably, the queue of impatient people waiting to be served hadn't received the memo. Fi felt more than conspicuous when she passed over her card and a note for five thousand pounds in cash.

'Er…' said the cashier. 'I'll have to ask a manager, Ms Booker.'

'I have the money,' said Fi. 'More to the point, it's *my* money.'

'Yes, but you're supposed to give us notice.'

'It's not that kind of account.'

'I mean generally. If you want more than two thousand pounds.'

'Why? Has the bank run out of money?'

'Ha ha!' The cashier forced a laugh. 'Tell you what, go into that booth and I'll fetch the manager.'

'I'm in a hurry,' said Fi. 'It's nearly lunchtime and I must . . . get back to relieve my staff.'

'I'm sure you do, but it's protocol. The manager won't be long.'

Keeping a smile plastered on her face, Fi went to sit in a booth that felt like a frosted goldfish bowl, aware that the people in the queue were looking at her. She wondered what they were thinking. Business loan to cover rising costs? Mortgaging the boat? Debt management? There was just enough signal to send Jade a message.

'Good morning, Ms Booker.' A young woman in a dark suit entered the goldfish bowl as she pressed *Send*. 'I'm Miss Smith, deputy manager. This shouldn't take long.'

'Good,' said Fi. 'I'm...' *Don't say you're in a hurry.* 'I'm sorry I didn't give any notice, but I have one of those bills where they don't take cards or bank transfer. Old-fashioned types.'

Miss Smith nodded, head on one side, calm but for eyes which bored into her. 'I imagine a lot of boating people are like that. Anti-bilging services?'

'Anti-fouling,' said Fi, automatically.

'Ah. We have to be careful.' Miss Smith tapped on a tablet to bring it to life. 'I have to confirm that you are not being coerced into giving someone money and that this is for legitimate services.'

'I just want some cash,' said Fi. 'I didn't think this sort of sum would be difficult.'

'Scammers are very clever,' said Miss Smith. 'The bank doesn't want to be held accountable if something goes wrong because we didn't check.'

'I want five thousand, not five million.'

'Good. I doubt we have that many used fivers.' Miss Smith grinned. 'If you can sign here, and here.' She watched Fi scrawl on the tablet's screen, then took it and trotted away. Fi wondered how anyone could legally tie her to the squiggle that was supposed to be her signature. Her palms were damp.

After what felt like a year, Miss Smith returned with an envelope full of twenty and fifty-pound notes, counted them out and handed them over. Stan got up and sniffed the air. '*Rrrerrfff?*' He pulled on his lead.

'Aww,' said Miss Smith, rubbing his ears. 'Are you being a brave dog and guarding mummy while she's carrying all that cash? Who's a good boy, then?'

Fi hurried outside, hampered by Stan. He was being difficult, pulling on the lead. She'd have to leave him at the boat while she went to the rowing club. There was just time, and it would allow her to message Jade again without anyone seeing.

Stan barked and dragged her straight into the path of Simon Davison.

'I'm so sorry,' she said.

'No harm done.' Simon rubbed his shoulder where they'd bumped into each other. Under his light summer jacket, his shirt was creased. 'I'm getting something for the hall. See you round, Fi. Take care.' He stalked into a small art gallery while Stan whined and pulled for home.

At the boat, she dug out a sturdy carrier bag and was about to stuff the money inside when she thought: *Do I really want to lose all this money? What if I try a double-bluff?* Her hands shook, but she filled the bag with brochures roughly the same size as bank notes, secured with elastic bands, and put one hundred pounds in twenties loose on the top before putting the remaining money in the safe. Then she put the carrier bag in her backpack and texted Jade to expect a review of the book very shortly. Jade would want everything in code, but there was no time to think of one. Sometimes the old-fashioned way was the only way. She scribbled a note to Jade:

Where we had a picnic the weekend before last while watching the racing is the place to be at noon today. Admittedly, where we put the wrappers afterwards, not the pretty bit. I'll be on high. If you still want to help, there should be plenty of safe cover. If you don't, I won't mind.

By the way, Zach is offering you website services too. Please tell him thanks and otherwise respond as you wish. Dispose of this, but don't eat it. My sensible side is gaining precedence.

She put it in a double envelope marked STRICTLY PRIVATE and went into the shop. 'Zach, can you go on your lunch break now, but first take this to Crystal Dreams and give it to Jade? It's about your offer to do website stuff for her. I can't promise she'll hire you, because her son's into that sort of thing, but she may know someone who will. I'd go, but I have to be somewhere else and I know you want me to ask. I promise we'll look at my website soon – I just need to clear the decks first.'

'Brilliant! Course I will.' Zach took the note and hurried off.

'I could have done that,' said Dylan, descending into the boat with cash for the main till.

'You'd have forgotten to go to Jade's and rushed off to pick Leo's brains,' said Fi, picking up her backpack. She couldn't meet her son's eyes. What would he think if he knew what she was doing? The sensible side was definitely gaining ground.

'I can pick Leo's brains if I want,' said Dylan. 'It's not—'

'Later, Dylan,' said Fi. 'I'm in a hurry.'

She ran onto the towpath. The sky was overcast, but if anything it was hotter than before. The rowing club was a good place for the blackmailer to pick, busy with people hiring boats, going for drinks in the bar, watching the rowers. Maybe this wasn't as amateurish as she'd thought. Fi's blood ran cold. Perhaps she should intercept Zach. And she shouldn't involve Jade in such a stupid idea—

Her phone buzzed. *Love the review. On the way to collect it.*

Fi made her way to the sailing club as quickly as possible. Trying not to look furtive, she dropped the bag in the bin as instructed, hoping the wrong person wouldn't pick it up. She rushed in the direction of home, then changed course in the middle of a flock of tourists and headed for a small, ancient riverside church. The verger was a loyal customer who would let her go on the bell tower's roof. It overlooked the river.

Fi climbed the worn steps, then knelt and peeped over the parapet. Despite her good head for heights, she began to feel queasy. Every urge to take risks dissolved.

Told you so, said her sensible brain, loudly.

Be quiet, Fi told herself. *It'll be over soon. All we have to do is wait.*

CHAPTER 16

How on earth do spies manage it? Jade checked her phone for the umpteenth time. Still no word from Fi. *Today is Tuesday, isn't it?* Well, according to her phone it was. She sighed and put her phone in her pocket.

'Are you all right?' asked Netta. 'You seem—'

'I'm fine,' said Jade. 'Do you want a brew?'

'No, thanks. I'll be heading out for my lunch fairly soon, anyway.'

'In that case, I'll get the kettle on,' said Jade. 'Otherwise I might not get a drink while you're out.'

'Fair point,' said Netta, looking at the queue. Admittedly, it wasn't stretching out of the door, but everyone had at least two items.

Jade went through to the back and switched the kettle on. She was pouring hot water into her mug when a tap at the door made her jump and splash it over the worktop. 'Jade?' said a timid voice.

'Yes, what?' snapped Jade. She put the kettle down, marched to the door and flung it open to be confronted by Fi's assistant, Zach. He was holding an envelope in front of him as if to ward her off.

'Fi asked me to give you this?' he said, holding out the envelope. Jade saw *STRICTLY PRIVATE* in Fi's writing.

'Thanks.' She grabbed it, closed the door, then ripped open the envelope, and the second one, and skimmed the note. 'Noon?' she muttered, and checked her phone. 'It's five to now!'

What to do, what to do? *I can't just run off*, she thought, attempting to take deep, slow breaths and failing completely. She opened the door and put her head round it. 'Netta, may I borrow you for a minute?'

'I'm serving,' said Netta.

'I need a word.'

Netta's eyebrows climbed up her forehead. 'Excuse me a moment,' she said to the customer she was serving, and walked towards the back room. In her head, Jade was urging her on. She held the door open for Netta, then closed it behind them.

'What's up?' said Netta.

'I need to pop out.'

Netta grinned. 'Did you get me in here just to tell me that?' Then the grin faded. 'What about my lunch

143

break?'

'You can still have your lunch break,' said Jade. 'Hopefully, I won't be too long. I'm not sure, though.'

'I'm supposed to finish in ten minutes,' said Netta. 'I mean, I could go later, but—'

'No, it's fine.' The last thing Jade felt like doing was negotiating with Netta. 'I'll be as quick as I can. If the shop's shut for five minutes, it doesn't matter. Not in the grand scheme of things.'

Suddenly, Netta frowned. 'Is this to do with the letter Zach brought?'

'Can't say,' said Jade. 'Anyway, I have to go, and the quicker I do, the quicker I'll be back.'

Netta gave her a suspicious look. 'Hope whatever it is goes OK,' she said, and opened the door. Jade nipped round her and walked quickly to the door which led up to her flat.

She hurried upstairs, her hair bouncing around her face. *I can't go like this. Why did I get those pink streaks put in? I might as well carry a placard saying 'Hello, I'm Fi's spooky friend.'*

She let herself in, ran to the bedroom and flung open the rickety wardrobe. On the top shelf was an old straw hat. Jade took off her long beaded necklace, which had a tendency to rattle, then gathered her hair into a big clip and rammed the hat on top. The only garment she could find unlike her other clothes, apart from the waxed jacket she had worn as a disguise once and which was far too hot for May, was a long cream cardigan. She pulled it on, sent a quick text to Fi, then grabbed a magazine for cover and rushed out.

The town was teeming with people, all intent on getting in her way. Jade weaved between them, trying not to curse under her breath. It seemed to take for ever to get to the cobbled street which led to the river. She fought the urge to run. Where was Fi? Was she on *Coralie*, or observing from somewhere else? *On high*, she had said.

The rowing club was round the next bend of the river. *Fi can't be on Coralie.* She had planned to stop at a bench outside the rowing club, but it was occupied. People were standing on the towpath in little groups, chatting, drinking from plastic glasses or paper cups, and generally obscuring the view. The terrace of the club was full of people having lunch or pre-lunch drinks and generally being loud and boaty.

Jade kept going. There was the bin, and she could see the bright flash of a plastic bag at the top. *They haven't picked it up yet. I'm in time. Where can I park myself?* She sidled through two groups of people who were too busy watching canoes gliding past to move out of the way, then risked a glance back. Everyone seemed to be looking at the river. But she was still too close.

Further on was another bench, unoccupied and quiet. Giving thanks to John Le Carre, or whoever the patron saint of spies was, Jade strolled casually towards it, sat down and opened her magazine.

Every time someone approached the bin she stiffened and glared round the edge of her magazine. But they only threw in paper cups or wrappers, then ambled off.

After ten minutes, she was bored. *All that rushing around for this. I'm glad I'm not a real spy: it must be so boring. If the James Bond films were true to life, we'd have to sit in the cinema for three hours watching Daniel Craig stare at a hollow tree.* Even so, she kept her magazine held up, turning the occasional page, but observing the bin all the while.

One of the groups on the towpath drifted away, followed a few minutes later by the other. A couple strolled by, and a young woman with a pushchair. Then came a man with a toddler on his shoulders. 'Let's count the ducks!' he said.

'One, two, three…' The toddler giggled.

A bead of sweat ran down Jade's back. *If I ever do this again, I'll make sure I get fair warning. It really isn't cardigan weather. At this rate I'll need a shower before I face the customers.* She wriggled, then turned the page.

Her phone buzzed and she jumped. Maybe Fi had somehow caught the blackmailers before they had even reached the bin. Maybe she'd given in and alerted Marcus, and some of the towpath drinkers were police officers in plain clothes. She found her phone.

The message was from Netta. *Hi Jade, I'm going on my lunch. I did wait, but it's gone quiet so it's a good time. See you soon I hope.*

Jade sighed, put the phone away and picked up her magazine. As she did, she felt hands on her shoulders.

'Don't move,' muttered a voice behind her.

Damn. I was so busy watching the bin that I never thought to look around me. Without moving her head, Jade managed sidelong glances along the towpath. No one was near, and the other side of the river was deserted.

'That's a good girl,' said the voice. 'Don't try anything, right?'

Jade risked a nod.

'Excellent,' said the voice. It wasn't a voice Jade had heard before. It would be quite deep for a woman and on the high side for a man, but it could have been either. The accent wasn't local, but Jade couldn't place it. *They're probably putting it on, anyway.*

'What are you doing?' she asked. *If you stall them, there's more chance someone will see you and come over.*

A laugh. 'You know exactly what we're doing. Well, what we *would* be doing if you weren't here. And you're not meant to be here. We told Fi she wasn't to tell anyone. That was a mistake.' A pause.

147

'Biiiig mistake.'

'Maybe Fi didn't tell anyone,' said Jade. 'Maybe I worked it out. There's no need to take it out on her.'

'Don't worry, we won't,' said the voice, and Jade could tell that the person, whoever they were, was smiling. 'Not directly.'

A boat was approaching rapidly from the left, the rowers straining at their oars. The boat almost seemed to lift from the water with every stroke. Further down the path, people were cheering.

'Impressive,' said the voice. 'Look at them go.'

The boat flashed past. The cheering grew louder.

'While everyone's watching that boat, no one's watching you. Fancy a trip, Jade?' Hands seized Jade's upper arms and forced her to her feet. 'That's it, up we go.'

She struggled, but her arms were in an iron grip. They marched her towards the river. 'Bet Fi never thought when she asked you to help that she'd end up getting arrested for your murder.'

Jade resisted and managed to turn slightly, but was pulled back. The water was inches away. *Can I swing round? Or throw myself backwards?* But she was being pushed further and further forward.

'Oi! Let go of her! What do you think you're doing?'

Suddenly the grip on her arms loosened and was gone. Jade wobbled on the edge of the path until

148

someone yanked her arm and she stumbled out of danger.

'Steady on,' said a voice she knew. Rick put his hands on her shoulders and guided her to the bench. 'Are you all right? What's going on?'

'It's a long story,' Jade gasped. She gazed at the towpath. Two running figures in jeans and T-shirts, with caps on their heads. 'I don't suppose you got a look at them, did you?'

'Not properly,' said Rick. 'I was focused on you. I heard you thundering downstairs a little while ago, which was odd, so I poked my head out and saw you hurrying off in a funny outfit. I thought, *She's up to something mysterious*, and as it was lunchtime I decided to take a look.'

'Thank heavens you did,' said Jade, and gave him a hug. Over his shoulder, she checked the bin. She could still see the carrier bag inside, and heaved a sigh of relief.

Rick gently freed himself. 'Are you sure you're not angry?'

Jade considered. She probably ought to be annoyed that Rick had invited himself along without asking. On the other hand, right now she was just grateful not to be fighting for her life in the river. 'Not at all,' she said. 'Thanks for watching out for me.'

'It isn't like you to rush out in the middle of the day when you have a business to run,' said Rick. 'And you're not the only one behaving strangely.'

'Really? Who else?' *At this rate, we'll have to invite Rick onto the team.*

'Well, I went out for a walk this morning before work and came across Simon from Spetisham Hall, moping about where that poor woman got drowned. He was poking around in the shrubbery with a stick. I don't know what he expected to find. I considered saying hello, but I decided he probably wouldn't be too pleased that someone had seen him.'

'No, I suppose not,' said Jade, her brain whirring. Was Simon involved somehow? Had his feelings for Bianca been a lie? Was he in on the blackmail? But Rick was saying something. 'I'm sorry, I was miles away,' she said.

'I was saying that we should get you back to the shop,' said Rick. 'You're probably in shock. I should head back, too. The pictures won't frame themselves.'

Jade opened her mouth to say that she was fine and he should go without her, then realised what a bad idea that was. The blackmailers had gone, but they could easily return. Suddenly, the safety of her shop and flat seemed like a very good idea. 'You're absolutely right. Just let me send a text first.'

It's time for Fi to tell Marcus what's going on, she thought, as her thumbs flew over the keyboard. *This has gone too far.*

CHAPTER 17

'What is it about "please leave crime to the police" that you two *still* don't get?' growled Marcus.

Fi hadn't needed Jade's text to contact him. She'd seen a commotion under the trees, then watched Rick and Jade embrace on the riverbank before walking towards town in a way that suggested Jade was more than happy to be escorted.

She'd messaged *Help* to Marcus, then run downstairs as quickly as the worn steps of the church tower would allow. She caught up with Jade, made sure she was unharmed, and let Rick take her home for a cup of restorative tea.

At that point, Marcus rang in a panic. Fi explained as simply as she could before collecting the carrier bag from the bin. It was sticky with ice-cream wrappers and fizzy-pop dregs, but the money and leaflets were safely inside.

A plain-clothes constable took statements at home from her, Jade and Rick, and an hour later, Marcus called again.

Fi had expected a reprimand, but all he'd asked was that she and Jade, travelling separately, meet him in a rundown greasy-spoon café in the county town of Wulfchester the next morning, on the grounds that it was hopefully the last place where anyone expected them to go. There, he would ask a few more questions.

They'd been there for half an hour. Marcus had painstakingly gone through their statements, shaking his head.

'It was a crime that might not have been a crime,' said Fi, before she could stop herself. She'd explained her thinking several times, each time feeling stupider, and couldn't believe that she was still arguing about such a ridiculous decision.

'A threat's a threat,' said Marcus. 'Some nasty yet harmless individual trying to wind you up is still harassment. I can't believe you didn't contact me the minute they asked for money. What if Jade had gone in the river? What if they'd attacked you?'

'I can swim,' said Jade. 'I got my fifty-metre badge at school.'

Marcus raised his eyebrows. 'With Doc Martens on? And even if you can swim, I'm reasonably sure Fi can't fly.'

'They couldn't have seen me go into the church.'

'You don't know that.'

'No, but—'

'Are you seriously still arguing that this was a good idea?'

'No.' Fi slumped in her seat and pushed her now-cold coffee away. A little sloshed into the saucer and onto the sticky Formica tabletop. 'I'm sorry, Jade. I shouldn't have involved you.'

'You shouldn't have involved yourself,' said Marcus.

'I'm a big girl,' said Jade. 'I can make my own decisions. But the decision I should have made was to ring Marcus myself when you got uncharacteristically spontaneous.'

'Hey! I can be spontaneous.'

'Prove it with something nice next time.' Jade's words were sharp but her voice was soft. She winked at Fi and managed a slightly wobbly smile. 'Please may I go, Mr Policeman? I've a shop to run. My assistant will either be fed up with me sloping off every five minutes, or using the opportunity to take Crystal Dreams down the revamp path of no return.'

'Yes, of course,' said Marcus. 'Just remember what I said. And maybe refresh those swimming lessons. Fully clothed.'

'Meh,' said Jade. 'The swans would have saved me. Or a witchy disinclination to sink.'

When she'd gone, Marcus and Fi sat in silence. With no air conditioner or extractor fan, the café was stifling. The air was full of steam from the coffee machine and greasy smoke from a grill and a sandwich toaster.

An elderly couple sat at another table, the man engrossed in the sports pages of a newspaper, the woman in a gossip magazine. An aged terrier lay with its head on the man's shoe, snoring. At another table, a gaggle of old ladies read out each other's horoscopes and shrieked with laughter over a radio station playing seventies classics.

Fi wished she'd brought Stan if Marcus was only going to admonish her. Perhaps she should ask for permission to go, too. But she didn't want to leave things like this.

'This'll never do,' said Marcus. He went to the counter and returned with a cup of tea for himself, a fresh cup of coffee for Fi and two packets of shortbread biscuits. 'Peace offering. I'd have got you a cinnamon whirl, but they look like dried-out cowpats.'

'Perhaps they are.'

Marcus stirred his cup of tea, which was a fraction lighter than mahogany, and Fi took a sip of the coffee. Even the froth burnt her tongue. 'What's this supposed to be?'

'Cappuccino. You should have had the tea. It was

made in a pot.'

'About two hours ago.'

'At least. There's nothing as insulating as a good tea cosy. You can keep a brew warm for days.'

'Yuck.' Fi sighed. 'I'm sorry I didn't tell you. I don't know what I was thinking.'

'You were thinking "It's all too personal and Marcus is being snippy with me".'

Fi pulled a face. 'Maybe. But that's an adolescent reaction. I'm an adult: I should have talked things through. I'm usually boringly sensible.'

'You're not boringly anything,' said Marcus, reaching for her hand. 'And it *is* personal and I *was* being snippy. But you should have told me.'

'I know.' She squeezed his fingers and picked up a packet of shortbread. 'The use-by date on this is three months ago.'

'That's fresh compared to what's in the police canteen,' said Marcus. 'It's sugar and flour, what could go wrong?'

'Ergot poisoning?'

Marcus opened his packet and dunked a biscuit in his tea. 'This'll burn off any urge to dance naked at midnight. Although maybe if someone sensible joined me…' His solemn face broke into a grin.

Fi grinned back, but her tension hadn't dissipated. 'I would have told you, but I didn't want to make you look stupid for wasting time investigating what might prove to be nothing. I thought people might accuse you of investigating because it was me, when you'd tell Mrs Bloggs not to worry. And yes, I was annoyed at how you spoke to me. Then . . . I suppose I got carried away. My anger at what Bianca alleged made me want to *do* something, not hand it over to someone else.' She bit her lip. 'You said I didn't know what Inspector Acaster was implying about you giving me leeway. Are you really getting stick because you and I go on dates sometimes?'

'Is that all we're doing?' Marcus sat back, his smile gone.

'I'm not going on dates with anyone else.'

'Glad to hear it. Nor me.'

'And I love it.'

'Good. Me too.'

'But honestly, are you getting stick?'

'Yup. Not just from other people. From myself, too.' Marcus dunked his biscuit again and the bottom half crumbled into his tea. 'Typical.'

'You'll have to eat it with the teaspoon,' said Fi. 'What do you mean, from yourself?'

'I feel as if I'm too close to be objective. I don't think for a moment that you'd kill anyone, for any reason. I don't even think you'd do it accidentally.'

'Even if you did, my alibi is sound.'

'It is. That doesn't mean you couldn't have instructed someone to kill Bianca. I don't believe that either.'

'I didn't know where she was staying. I wasn't even sure of her last name. I had to dredge it from my memory.'

'That name isn't coming up anywhere and tracking down her relations is proving tricky.'

'Simon gave it to me. Presumably it was what he knew her as at university.'

'He told us too, but said she changed it informally after graduating because she'd fallen out with her father. So far, checking where she's been – including Italy – is proving even trickier. If she was carrying her passport, it's in the river now. Otherwise… Anyway, I believe you. It's just – I worry that my instincts as a police officer are being overshadowed by how I feel about you. I need to investigate, and at the same time, it feels as if I'm intruding on your privacy. I'd back off, only Nina Acaster's next in line. She's bad enough when she isn't recovering from summer flu.'

Fi felt her face warm, and realised her heart had warmed too. 'If you have to hand it over, Marcus, I understand. I can cope with Inspector Acaster.'

'Why should you have to cope? Sometimes a risk is worth taking.' He wagged a finger. 'And sometimes it isn't.'

'I wouldn't feel so bad if it weren't for what nearly happened to Jade.'

'What about me?' said Marcus. 'How do you think

I feel when you don't tell me stuff? And it's hard knowing that this is linked to you even though you're innocent. In fact, you're a victim. If I'd known about the blackmail, we could have put trackers on the money, then intercepted them. I believe your instinct that the blackmailer is an amateur is right. It might have been a quick sting, and all over by now.'

'At least you have some leads.'

'I suppose so. Come on, let's get out of here. I need fresh air. I can't work out if I'm going to die from lack of a cheese toastie, or whether I never want to smell one again.'

'I know what you mean.'

They went outside. The sun beat down but it felt less oppressive, the air more breathable.

'I'm sorry,' said Marcus. 'I didn't mean to be snippy with you the other day. It came out wrong.'

'I'm sorry too,' said Fi. 'I didn't set out to be secretive: I overreacted. I think it's living with a teenager. All that moodiness is catching.'

'That's the other thing,' said Marcus, staring after a small car being driven at speed by a youth. 'Leo's a worry. He barely talks to his mother and he's plain rude to me. I don't know what he's up to. Or even who he's with, half the time.'

'Have you tried the skate park, or fast-food places?' said Fi. 'Leo met up with Dylan at one of them to pick his brains about something. Exams, I assume.'

Marcus stared at her. 'Exams? I doubt Leo remembers anything he did for GCSE, and none of the subjects he's doing for AS level would appeal to Dylan. It's hard to say that my son may not be the best influence on yours, but...'

'It'll be nothing,' said Fi. 'Leo's a nice kid. Dylan's a nice kid. We're just their parents, and right now they're making dramas where there aren't any. Dylan wants to play music on the deck of *Coralie* in a few weeks' time – didn't you say that one of Leo's friends has a good PA system? Otherwise, I expect they were whinging about us.'

'Hope so,' said Marcus. 'In the meantime, will you promise not to go off investigating without me?'

'Promise.' Fi sniffed her shoulder. 'I think I smell of grilled cheese.'

Marcus bent to kiss her. 'You smell all right to me,' he said. 'Next time, let's go somewhere a bit more upmarket, OK?'

CHAPTER 18

Jade made a face as she put in a second silver moon earring. *I'm not sure if I'm under or overdressed. But hey, it's a night out. And if it wasn't for Rick, I might not be alive to worry over appropriate attire for the Four Feathers.*

She surveyed herself in the mirror. The Feathers had a reputation for being a bit of a dive, so getting dolled up seemed ridiculous. On the other hand, she was going to a gig, and had been invited by a member of the band. There were several options, ranging from jeans and T-shirt at one end to floaty dresses at the other. *I'll feel worse if I'm overdressed*, she told herself firmly, settling the waistband of her jeans and adjusting the neckline of her floaty top. *Besides, I need to wear practical things, like footwear I can run in.* She recalled the hated heels, now residing at the back of her wardrobe, and grimaced.

She texted Fi. *Heading out to the Feathers. Rick said it would finish at half ten and he'd walk me home, so should be back by 11 at latest. I'll text when I am.* She pressed *Send* and stuffed the phone in her jeans pocket.

The Four Feathers was the sort of pub you needed to have been told about, since it was down an alley, left into another, then up some steps. Jade walked cautiously, glad it was still light.

At least Rick had given her permission to skip the first half. 'I mean, you could come,' he had said, his face conveying that it would be a bad idea. 'The new bands, they do need an audience. But a lot of them will bring their friends and family. And there's only so many covers of "Fairytale of New York" that you can listen to in one evening.'

'Really?' said Jade. 'Have to admit, you aren't selling it to me.'

'Or me,' said Netta, who had brought in her laptop and was hunched behind the counter, typing.

Jade wondered whether Netta's business case would ever be presented. Then again, that had partly been her motive for requesting one. As she watched Netta frown, type, consult her notebook and type some more, she did feel rather bad. However, Jade had taken on all customer service and stock replenishment while Netta was busy building her imaginary empire, so they were both mugs.

But at least it kept her mind off a range of things: nearly being thrown in the river, not getting so much as a glimpse of the blackmailers, and poor Fi's predicament. Hopefully, though, Fi and Marcus were reconciled. Maybe it would even bring them closer together. Wasn't stress and adrenaline meant to do that, like taking your intended to a scary movie or on a ghost train? Then she recalled her own recent ordeal. 'I've got more sense,' she muttered.

'Sorry?' said Rick.

Jade remembered where she was and with whom. 'Oh, I've got more sense than to come early,' she said hurriedly. 'Are you in the second half?'

'We're headlining,' said Rick, with a little smile. 'We'll be on from about nine.' He handed Jade a folded piece of paper. 'Here's your ticket.'

LIVE AT THE FOUR FEATHERS!!!
THE WAYFARERS
THE ROGUES
SOUTHPORT CONVENTION
DEATH ROW TULL
PLUS MANY MORE!!!

'Wow, top of the bill,' she said, putting it in her pocket. 'That'll be a collectors' item when you're properly famous.'

'We'll all be dead before that happens,' said Rick, and immediately looked contrite. 'Sorry, I didn't mean – what with—'

'Don't worry, Rick, absolutely fine,' said Jade, glancing in Netta's direction and putting a finger to her lips. Luckily, Netta was deep in the mysteries of her document. 'I'll see you later.'

'Lovely. I'll let you and Mary Portas there crack on.'

'Who's Mary Portas?' asked Netta.

'A retail guru.' Netta still looked puzzled. 'Oh, never mind.'

***

As Jade had expected, the Four Feathers was rammed. She squeezed through the crowd as the strains of 'The Irish Rover' grew slightly louder before coming to an abrupt halt she didn't remember in the original song.

'And for the grand finale, "Fairytale of New York"!' bellowed the singer, hanging on to the microphone stand as if it was the only thing keeping him upright. 'You can all sing along!' Some of the clientele started immediately, and Jade decided she would need a drink.

It took her a few minutes to get to the bar, partly because the crowd around it was two deep and partly because her Doc Martens were sticking to the floor. *Into the shower with you later, my girl*, she told herself.

Finally, she reached the bar. 'Rum and Coke, please,' she hollered over the din, putting her elbows on the bar then wishing she hadn't.

'Coming up, love,' the bartender shouted. He seemed to be juggling several orders, and she watched him pull pints, shovel ice in glasses, and pour a brimming glass of red wine. 'Double whiskey on the rocks, large Rioja, pint of Doom Bar!'

'Got a tray?' Jade glanced in the speaker's direction and was surprised to see Simon. She was about to say hello when she remembered what Rick had said about him snooping around the crime scene. Hastily, she turned away and waited for perhaps half a minute. When she looked again, his blue chambray back was progressing carefully towards the rear of the pub.

Not here for the gig. Interesting.

Shortly afterwards, the bartender put down her drink. 'Sorry for the wait,' he said. 'It's a madhouse. The Rogues are very popular.'

'I can tell,' said Jade, touching her card to the reader and trying not to wince as the audience gave each other their best Shane MacGowan. 'How about the Wayfarers?'

He shrugged. 'Haven't heard them before. They've been going a while, though, so they should be decent. Otherwise they'd have broken up.' He grinned. 'Who's next?'

On impulse, Jade shook her hair over her face, then took her drink and wandered to the back of the pub.

164

Simon was putting down drinks at a corner table. The glass of Rioja was for a petite woman with an explosion of dark curls. Jade could only see part of her profile but she looked thirtyish, with olive skin. She was wearing a denim jacket, but so was half the pub.

Simon put the whiskey in front of— 'I don't believe it,' murmured Jade, tightening her grip on her glass.

The Gavinalike! It had to be. She could have picked him out of a lineup, based on the photos Fi had shown her. It was all she could do not to elbow her way through the crowd and shout 'What sort of husband are you?' Except that he wasn't Fi's husband. Unless he was.

Simon put the pint on the table, slipped the tray underneath, and sat down with his back to her. *Good. He's the only one of the three who might expect to see me.* She longed to sidle over and eavesdrop. After her recent experience, though, she satisfied herself with leaning on a pillar five feet away, mostly watching the band – or as much of it as she could glimpse through the press of spectators – but occasionally casting a quick glance at the table.

The Gavinalike actually had his head in his hands, and Simon didn't look much happier. The woman was talking with animation and gesturing, but the Gavinalike was shaking his head.

The next time Jade peeped, Simon seemed marginally happier but the woman's glass was half empty. *Careful*, thought Jade. *I know all about big glasses of wine.*

Then it hit her. *What if this gang are the blackmailers? They could be. Maybe Bianca was having second thoughts and they decided they had to kill her.* She felt herself stiffen and resolved to stay till the end of the gig, even if it was awful, so that Rick could walk her home.

At long last, 'Fairytale of New York' ground to a noisy halt. The crowd roared and stamped in approval. 'Again!' someone shouted.

'We'd love to,' said the lead singer, 'but our time is up.'

'Ohhh,' the crowd whined.

'Never mind. Get yourself a drink before the headliners come on. We'll be at the bar, so you can buy us one too!'

The crowd cheered, and Jade flattened herself against the pillar as they rushed to the bar. For some reason, the PA system started playing 'Chain Reaction'.

Behind her, a chair scraped. Jade glanced over her shoulder. The woman was getting up. Quickly, she turned away. 'Ciao,' the woman called, and went on her way.

Jade peeled herself off the pillar and followed at a

distance. Was she heading to the bar? No. She passed it and made for the exit.

I can't follow her. I'll miss the gig, and besides, it may be a trap. Nevertheless, she kept going, using the wake through the spectators that the woman had made.

She reached the door, which was propped open, in time to see the woman heading down the alley. She looked full of confidence. *Definitely suspicious.*

'Wouldn't have thought that was *her* scene,' remarked one of a couple drinking at a table outside.

'Excuse me,' said Jade, 'do you know her? It's just that she's left her scarf behind. I'd go after her, but I don't want to miss the Wayfarers.'

'Yeah, that's Liv Fratelli,' said the man. 'I'd have said Europop was more her thing.' He and the woman brayed with laughter.

'Thanks,' said Jade. 'I'll put the scarf behind the bar and tell them whose it is.' She went back in, reflecting that perhaps there was a good reason why Liv Fratelli had turned to the dark side. *Anyway, time for some fun.*

As so many people were still at the bar, Jade managed to secure a stool near the front, with a little ledge to put her drink on. The Wayfarers were tuning up. Rick saw her as he was turning this way and that to talk to the rest of the band, between frowning at the neck of his guitar and adjusting pegs. He raised a hand in greeting, then leaned over to one of his bandmates and murmured in his ear.

Are they talking about me? Jade felt her face heat up and hoped she wasn't turning red. Then again, the pub was pretty warm.

She pulled out her phone. At least now she didn't have to worry that Marcus and his colleagues were bugging it. *You won't believe this*, she typed. *Simon and the Gavinalike are drinking together in the 4 Feathers. There was a woman too. Dark curly hair, maybe 30s, she's just left. Someone outside said her name was Liv Fratelli. Ring any bells?*

Fi's reply came a minute later. *Don't I repeat DON'T get close or follow any of them. And yes, Fratelli sounds familiar. Enjoy the gig, and if Rick can't take you home, phone me. Or Marcus.*

What do you take me for? replied Jade.

'Right, let's get started,' said Rick. 'We are the Wayfarers and we're a folk band, but sometimes we diversify. Here's an example. Get your hands in the air for 10CC's "I'm Not in Love", with a twist!'

The people still at the bar turned their heads, then ambled towards the stage. Rick winked at Jade. 'A-one-two-three-four!'

I'm not reading anything into that. He's being silly. But she had to admit, as the harmonies soared above the heads of the swaying audience, that he was making a pretty good job of it. *Hopefully we are, too.*

She imagined the tentacles of justice reaching out to grab the blackmailers. *They're within our grasp now,* she thought, and smiled.

CHAPTER 19

'Someone wants your help with the best books on Italy,' whispered Zach. 'I can take over here.'

Fi's heart missed a beat as she gave a brief apology to the person she was serving and looked across the boat. But the customer standing by the travel section, a short balding man in his fifties, was someone she knew, the owner of a tasteful souvenir shop.

'Good morning, Alan,' she said. 'Italy, is it?'

'Silver wedding anniversary,' he said, as if discussing a prison sentence. 'I like Mallorca but Sue wants Italy. Doesn't pay to argue. I need ideas.'

'What sort of place?'

'Full board, flashy, view, food, entertainment.' Alan seemed even gloomier.

'Here you are,' said Fi, picking out a book. 'This has information on everything from bijou to grand.'

'I was thinking of a nice quiet family-run place.

Romantic, like what started the conversation.'

'Sorry?'

'Vecchia Pescara. We went for a meal there last Saturday. Tony was talking—'

'Tony Fratelli? Of course!'

'Of course?'

Fi dragged her mind into focus. 'It's a great restaurant – haven't been for ages. Now, is the book OK?'

Once Alan Andrews had gone, Fi messaged Marcus, telling him that a Liv Fratelli seemed to know both Simon and the man who'd been seen by the river. Then she messaged Jade: *Fancy a takeaway pizza? Tony Fratelli sells the best at Vecchia Pescara down Tudor Lane. 12?*

Within seconds, Jade responded. *It's a bit early, but yes, if you're paying.*

They met just before midday in the cobbled lane outside the restaurant. 'You're not planning on hiding behind a potted plant to spy, are you?' said Jade. 'They might not be related at all.'

'Just a simple question or two and we'll see what happens,' said Fi. 'And yes, I've told Marcus.'

They entered the takeaway area. The restaurant beyond was already busy, with serving staff moving between customers in a dainty-footed dance. The chatter sounded happy, the words indistinguishable under soft classical music.

'I can't believe I didn't know this was here,' said Jade, perusing the menu. 'Why didn't you tell me?'

'We've always gone to a pub, haven't we? This is good for dates. By the way, how did the rest of yesterday evening go?'

'Why?' Jade's eyes narrowed.

Fi was startled by the sharpness of her response. 'I heard it was a good gig with a good vibe and wondered if you thought the same.'

'Oh. Yes, it was great.' Jade buried herself in the menu again, then looked up. 'Is this Tony coming over?'

'Yes, that's him.' Fi smiled as a middle-aged man in smart chinos and a dark-blue linen shirt arrived. He seemed as if he ought to be lounging on a superyacht in the French Riviera, not running a restaurant.

'Good day, ladies! Ms Booker, so delightful to see you again, and this time with a friend! In fact . . . am I right in thinking you're Ms Fitch of Crystal Dreams?'

'Erm, yes.'

'My wife loves your shop. Delighted to meet you. Now then, ladies, what would you like?'

'Quattro stagioni, please, to take away,' said Jade.

'I'll have a margherita, please,' said Fi.

'Coming right up.'

'I'll have to bring my son here,' said Jade, when Tony returned in what seemed like no time with two neat pizza boxes. 'He loves good authentic cuisine and yours looks excellent. I'm sorry we're getting a takeaway, but our lunch breaks are short.'

'All this rushing lunch is bad for people,' said Tony, shaking his head. 'I keep telling my daughter, but will she listen?'

'My son would agree with you,' said Jade. 'He likes nothing better than a leisurely meal with good music and fine wine.'

'When you want to bring him, Ms Fitch, let me know and I'll prepare a feast! And perhaps you will introduce him to my Livia so that he can convert her. Rush rush, sticky pubs, rubbishy music, late nights… Last night, for example, and what happens? Sooo tired when she goes to work today.'

'Oh no!' said Fi, hoping she looked concerned rather than excited. 'Where does she work?'

Tony shrugged with the entire top half of his body. 'She has a good job. Today, she is at the college. Anyway, *buon appetito*! Let's hope this is the first of many visits, Ms Fitch. Ms Booker, I look forward to you returning soon with your *other* friend.' He winked.

Fi could still sense Jade's smirk and feel her face burning when they'd left the lane. She ignored both. 'Let's go to the college.'

'What about the pizza?'

'You can eat yours in the car. I'll heat mine up later.'

'What will we say when we get there? Didn't we promise to leave this to Marcus? Didn't *you* promise to return to being Ms Words O'Wisdom?'

Fi typed a message and sent it. 'There, I've told him. He hasn't replied to the last one yet.'

'The Chief Constable probably confiscates their phones if they answer personal messages on duty.'

'We're on to something,' said Fi. 'I'm sick of lying awake at night because someone is trying to ruin my life. I'm sick of threats, of looking over my shoulder, of worrying about my friends and arguing with Marcus. If Liv Fratelli is an Italian link to Bianca and behind this whole sorry mess...' She took a deep breath. 'All I want to do is look her in the eye and let her know we're on to her. Hopefully, by then, Marcus will have read my messages, done some digging and be ready to take over. I'm not interfering with an investigation: I'm one of the victims.'

'All right, all right,' said Jade. 'Let's get cracking before her father tells her we were in the restaurant asking after her.'

It was only a short drive to the college. Unlike on the open day, the visitors' car park was fairly empty. With Jade in tow, Fi marched to reception, rehearsing her speech in her head.

'Hello,' she said to the receptionist. 'I know it's lunchtime, but I wonder if it's possible to speak with Liv Fratelli. It's a—'

'Liv Fratelli?' The receptionist looked blank and half-turned to a colleague who was bringing a mug of tea. 'Which course is she on?'

'She's not a student,' said the colleague, tapping on a list. 'I'll get her. She'll be in the staffroom having lunch, I expect.'

'Oh,' said the receptionist. 'I never thought. Take a seat, ladies, she'll be along shortly.'

Fi paced, looking at the displays of artwork on the walls without taking them in. They'd delighted her when she'd come with Zach. Now the walls might as well have been blank. Finally, she could confront the woman Bianca must have worked with, who could confirm if the man was Gavin or not. She knew that Jade, clutching her beads like a talisman, was wary, but at least they were in public.

'Hi, can I help you? I'm Liv.'

Fi turned and saw a petite woman in a green jumpsuit, her pretty brown-eyed face framed by dark curls. Then Liv noticed Jade. 'You were at the gig last night, weren't you? I remember thinking how nice your hair was. Were the Wayfarers good? I would have stayed, but—'

'Things were getting emotional?' said Fi, hearing her voice harden.

Liv blinked. 'Not for me. Were you there too?'

'You were comforting someone,' said Jade. 'He seemed upset.'

'He was, poor man,' said Liv. 'I could only help him so much, then I had to go. A colleague needed help with an emergency. Shame, I was looking forward to the Wayfarers.'

Fi frowned. Was Liv lying? She seemed genuine. 'Wasn't the man a friend?'

'Never seen him before in my life,' said Liv. 'I started talking to him because he was muttering in Italian and clearly upset. I could understand him and I figured no one else could. He said "No one can help me now. I should never have got involved".' I couldn't get him to explain before I had to go. Perils of the job!' She laughed and tapped the badge pinned to her outfit. *Liv Fratelli, Special Constable.*

Fi suddenly took in the information screen by the entrance. *Careers Fair Today!*

'I told my boss, though,' Liv continued. 'Since it was an odd thing to say. Speak of the devil, here he is. Are you coming to help, sir? I didn't know we were getting anyone so senior. The kids will love it – but you'll get a million questions about murder.'

Fi turned and saw Marcus. His expression was neutral, but she knew him well enough to recognise his deep irritation.

'These ladies were at the gig last night and worried about that chap I mentioned,' said Liv, smiling then checking her watch. 'Ten minutes to kick off, sir. Do you want me to show you where we're set up?'

'Please,' said Marcus. 'While you do that, these ladies can return to their business. As quickly as possible.'

Fi and Jade returned to town in silence. Fi dropped Jade off, sensing every unspoken word her friend was thinking, then parked and made her way to the boat. It had seemed so simple. What had she done?

Deep in miserable thoughts, she entered the boat. She was halfway through the shop before she realised that Nerys was looking anxious and heard the ominous thud of bass coming from the private quarters.

'The post came just after you left,' said Nerys. 'A letter for Dylan and this one for you.' She handed over a familiar envelope. 'Dylan read his and went peculiar. Stomped into the private area and turned his music up. I asked him if he wanted to talk about it, but he wouldn't. The noise is putting people off and I don't know what to do.'

'Thanks, Nerys,' said Fi, feeling suddenly sick. 'Get yourself and Zach a cup of tea from Willow's while I talk to him. Close the shop and have a break on deck.'

Dylan was sitting at the table, head down, a letter crumpled in his hand. Fi sat next to him and waited. He lifted his head, his face streaked with tears, and threw the screwed-up letter at her.

Fi flattened it out. In those familiar stencilled

177

letters, it said: *Where's your dad? Are you sure he's dead?*

'Are you one of those mothers who won't let their children see their own fathers?'

'No, of course not! Dylan—'

'It's like Leo said. The more upstanding the parent seems, the more of a hypocrite they are. I bet you've been lying to me my whole life. You care more about this boat than you do about me.'

'Dylan—'

'You don't understand *anything*, Mum. Just go away and run your business. That's all you care about. I want to be alone.' He gave her a cold, miserable glare, snatched up his phone and earbuds and stomped into his cabin.

She half rose to follow him, then sank into the chair. *Let him be*, she told herself. *He needs space. When he's calmed down, he'll talk – he always has before. At least he hasn't gone off to town. I'm not letting them get between us.*

She sighed, and with trembling fingers opened her own letter.

We told you not to involve anyone else. This time, pay attention. Get £20,000 ready for when we get in touch again. If you mess this up, maybe your son will be reunited with his father at last. Since I doubt he trusts you any more, there'll be nothing you can do to stop that happening.

178

CHAPTER 20

Jade was putting out stock for the next day when her phone buzzed. 'Hang on,' she muttered. She unpacked the final cauldron and set it carefully on the shelf. Next to it, she placed a set of silver measuring spoons. 'There.' She stepped back to admire the effect, then reached into her pocket.

The message was from Fi. *Bad news. Another letter. They sent one to Dylan, too. He's beside himself.*

Jade's eyes nearly jumped out of her head. *How dare they! Do you want me to come round?* In preparation, she fetched her coat.

'Are we closing early?' said Netta.

'Depends,' said Jade, watching her phone.

It buzzed again. *It's OK. Well, it isn't, but Marcus is here. I rang him as soon as I read the letters. They've been taken for analysis. I'm trying to talk to*

Dylan. I'll text if I need anything, but thanks x

Make sure you do. Thinking of you x. Jade put her phone away and heaved a sigh.

'Are you all right?' asked Netta. 'That pizza wasn't funny, was it? You hardly touched it.'

'It was fine. You can have it if you like.'

Netta wrinkled her nose. 'You're OK.' She gave Jade an odd look. 'I was wondering…'

'What were you wondering?'

Netta went to her bag and took out a folder. 'I got my business case printed out at the library.'

Jade held out her hand and Netta put the folder in it. She drew out the document, which was thicker than she had anticipated. 'OK, I'll read it tonight.'

Netta clapped her hands, bouncing up and down a little. 'Oh, I'm so excited!'

Jade raised her eyebrows. 'I might say no.'

'But I did it. I wrote a business case. Freddy Stott would never have let me do that. He only hired me because I was cheap. Well, there was another reason, but I made it clear he had no chance.'

'Glad to hear it,' said Jade, grimacing. 'Netta, it's quarter past five. Why don't you head off?'

'Really?'

'Yes, really. It's quiet, and I can handle anyone who comes in.' *I hope.*

'Great!' Netta straightened up the counter and collected her things. 'I'll tell Hugo you're reading my business case.'

Jade raised an eyebrow. 'Has he seen it?'

Netta looked cagey. 'He has. He didn't write any of it.'

'Good, because I'd spot him a mile off. If there's anything in there about spiffing offers or echoing funnels, I'll know.'

Netta giggled. 'I'll tell him that too.'

'Be my guest. You're still talking to each other, then?'

'Yeah,' said Netta, as if that was obvious. 'We're watching *Only Murders In The Building* together tonight.'

Jade frowned. 'How do you—'

'We start watching at the same time and message each other,' Netta explained. 'Hugo reckons he knows who did it, but he's wrong.' She slung her bag on her shoulder. 'Will you text me?'

'Text you?'

'About the business case.'

'I'll tell you tomorrow.'

Netta's eyebrows knitted. 'What if it's busy?'

'Goodnight, Netta.'

Once she had cashed up, Jade took herself and the business case up to the flat. She made a strong cup of tea, got the emergency biscuits from the cupboard, and settled on the sofa.

Magic in Cyberspace: Taking Crystal Dreams

Online, she read.

'Good grief,' muttered Jade. She put the document on the sofa and sipped her tea.

There must be something I can do for Fi, she thought.

Don't be silly. Fi's priority is Dylan right now, and Marcus is there. You'd get under their feet.

She sighed, fished the remote from its special place down the side of the sofa cushion and switched on the TV. On *Wyvernshire Tonight*, Martin Marsden was speaking seriously about the impact of littering.

Jade snorted. 'I bet you don't mean corpses and boathooks,' she muttered, and switched over. She took a biscuit and flipped to the first page of Netta's business case.

Crystal Dreams is a very successful crystals and magic shop set in the heart of the bustling market town of Hazeby-on-Wyvern.

I'm not flogging the shop, Netta! Jade turned the page to find a line graph with alarming peaks and troughs. She shuddered and put it aside.

What will I do with myself? Fi was, quite understandably, occupied. Hugo would be doing a watchalong with Netta. And Rick…

You saw Rick last night. Anyway, you don't want to go there. He's nice enough, but men are trouble. Look at the mess Fi's in.

Jade got up and fetched the pizza box from the

fridge. She had eaten a slice in Fi's car on the way to the college, but afterwards it hadn't appealed. She opened the lid and looked at it, then shrugged, slid it on a plate and put it in the oven to heat.

Not all men are trouble. Besides, here you are, alone, heating up cold pizza. Hardly winning at life, is it?

'Shut up,' Jade muttered. 'I saw him yesterday.'

There's nothing to be ashamed of in liking someone.

Jade growled. *You're supposed to be on my side.*

I am. Frankly, I don't think you're doing yourself any favours. Rick's a nice guy. Would it hurt to reach out to him?

Zing! went the TV. A contestant answered a question.

He's probably out, thought Jade.

So text him and find out.

And what if Fi needs me? What do I do then?

Fine. Suit yourself. So Jade ate pizza in front of the TV, allowed herself a small glass of wine, and completely failed to read Netta's business case.

She slept surprisingly well. A little too well, hitting the snooze button then struggling awake at eight fifteen. After a frenetic dash around the flat to get ready, she arrived downstairs at quarter to nine clutching a piece of toast.

Netta was already in and neatening the shelves.

183

'What do you think?' she asked.

'About what?'

Netta smiled. 'The business case!' The smile faded. 'You did read it, didn't you?'

'Of course,' said Jade. 'I need to reread it before I can make a decision, though.'

'Oh. I can serve while you read it.'

'I left it upstairs.'

'Shall I put the kettle on while you fetch it?'

'Thanks.' Jade trudged upstairs, wondering why the world was being mean to her, and returned with the document. A steaming mug was waiting on the counter.

'You can go in the back,' said Netta. 'I'll give you a shout if it gets busy.'

The shop had been open less than ten minutes when Jade was summoned. In any case, she had heard raised voices in the shop and was itching to know what was going on.

The three witches were standing together at the counter. 'The Book Barge has been attacked!'

Jade stared at them, her blood running cold. 'Attacked?'

'Someone's painted *LIAR* on the side in big red letters,' said the first witch. 'It must have happened overnight. I was walking my cat along the towpath this morning and I saw the owner outside, talking to a police officer. I suppose she won't be able to clean it off until they've done fingerprints or tests or whatever they do.'

Jade's fists clenched. *Poor Fi. As if blackmail isn't enough.*

'Isn't she your friend?' said the second witch. 'The boat's owner. Fi, isn't it? I must say, I've always found her prices fair.'

'I doubt it's a dissatisfied customer,' said Jade.

'No,' said the second witch. 'Do you have a sense of who it could be? Maybe if you did some visualising—'

'I'll think about it,' said Jade. 'In the back room.'

She sat down at the table and put her head in her hands. Then she texted Fi. *I've just heard what happened to Coralie. Are you all right? Please say and I can come straight round. Or whatever.*

She stared at Netta's business case while she waited for a response, taking nothing in.

A few minutes later, her phone buzzed.

Good news travels fast, eh. Don't worry, the police know and someone's cleaning it off right now. Luckily they used emulsion, so it isn't too bad.

Jade's fingers flew over the keyboard. *If there's anything I can do…*

Fi's reply came by return. *Thanks.*

Jade managed another half hour in the back room, then decided she would go stir crazy if she had to look at the business case any longer. She took it into the shop and put it in the counter drawer. 'Right, who's next?'

Jade kept herself busy, but as she chatted with customers, recommended products and put out more stock, her mind whirled. They'd drawn a blank with Liv Fratelli, but what about Simon and the Gavinalike? What had he said – 'I should never have got involved'? That sounded like a guilty conscience talking. But could they prove it? And surely, if there had been anything dodgy, Liv the special constable would have reported it.

'Do you mind if I go for lunch?' asked Netta. She glanced at the drawer.

'That's fine,' said Jade. 'And yes, I will give you an answer before the end of the day.'

Netta headed out.

Jade served the rest of the queue, then looked around the shop. For once, it was empty. She leaned on the counter and pondered.

This doesn't add up. There's blackmail, and then… Why would someone write LIAR on Fi's boat?

Maybe it's not connected with blackmail.

Pull the other one, it's got bells on. Of course it is! Fi's never had any trouble before, and now… But why write 'liar'? If they'd written slut or floozy, because of Marcus, that would make sense. It would probably hurt Fi more. But liar…

Jade racked her brains. Something was there, but it

wouldn't come… While the shop was quiet she took out Netta's document, hoping it might jog her memory. She scanned page after page, but couldn't take anything in. *You've done a great job, Netta. I wish I was in a state to appreciate it.*

A customer came in, and Jade was kept busy serving until Netta's return. Immediately, she saw the document. 'Have you…?'

'I'm just having one more look.'

'I'll make tea,' said Netta, her voice neutral.

'One second,' Jade said to the woman next in line. She paged through the document and a heading caught her eye: *Implementation and costings.*

Various online shop fronts are available. Some options offer a free trial—

Bingo! 'I've done it!' she called as Netta returned with a mug of tea, looking downcast. 'What's up?'

'If it isn't good enough, you can say,' said Netta. 'I'm a big girl. I can take it.'

'Don't be daft,' said Jade. 'I've had a lot on my mind today, that's all. Anyway, I propose a trial. Here's the deal: you set up a shopfront for a month with limited stock, using as many free trials as you can find. I'll set a budget, and we'll see how it goes.'

'Really?' Netta put the mug down so quickly that tea slopped on the counter.

'Yes,' said Jade. 'You can start next week. Now, come and serve this customer. I need my lunch too.'

She put Netta's document in the drawer, then headed towards the door to her flat.

'How can I help you?' asked Netta.

The woman let out a wheezy chuckle. 'I'm throwing a surprise party for my sister and it's going to have a magical theme!'

'Oh, wow!' exclaimed Netta. 'You've come to the right place, then.'

'It will be such fun! I've sent out the invitations and told everyone not to breathe a *word* to Marnie. In fact, I said they mustn't tell *anyone*!' She giggled. 'And of course, I haven't told Marnie.'

Jade paused, her hand on the door handle. *They mustn't tell anyone... Where have I heard something similar?* She shook her head and went upstairs.

Halfway up, she froze, then smacked her forehead. *Of course – the blackmailer's first letter! 'The things you haven't told anyone'!*

'I'm an idiot,' she said aloud, then ran upstairs, let herself in, and flopped on the sofa.

She grabbed her phone and texted Fi. *About the graffiti – I've had a thought. In the first letter, the blackmailer said something like 'things you haven't told anyone'. What do they mean?*

She pressed *Send* and dropped the phone on the sofa, then put her head back and sighed out a breath. She winced as she remembered that she had approved Netta's business case, then relaxed. *I'll set her a small budget and make sure she uses existing stock. A month can't hurt. Besides, Netta will be so worried about failing that she'll be extra careful.* She smiled. *And Hugo will look after her.*

She stayed where she was, taking deep, slow breaths, but something still niggled at her.

Her eyebrows drew together and she sat up. *Fine. What the heck.* She picked up the phone, found Rick's last message, and hit *Reply.*

I'm heading out for lunch. Want me to get food and bring it round?

The message was marked as read. Then three dots appeared and jiggled up and down.

Maybe he's busy, she thought. *Maybe he's got a sandwich.*

The three dots vanished and Jade huffed. Then they reappeared, followed shortly after by: *That would be great. I'll get the kettle on. I eat pretty much anything.*

Jade grinned. *Glad to hear it*, she replied. She bounced off the sofa and headed downstairs.

CHAPTER 21

The things you haven't told anyone. Fi put her phone in her pocket. Jade was right. That phrase must be relevant – but what did it mean?

Marcus had arranged for the letters to be collected surreptitiously the previous day. He had also told Fi to give every indication that she was going along with the blackmail and hadn't told the police.

The graffiti had been a horrible shock. For a brief, treacherous moment, Fi wondered if Dylan was responsible or had got someone else – maybe Leo – to do it. When she saw his face, though, she knew for certain he'd done neither. He went pale, his fists clenching as he swore. Then he whispered 'How dare they?' and ran his hand over *Coralie*'s door frame. 'Why, Mum?'

'Not because it's true,' said Fi. She felt close to tears and the words were hard to get out. She realised she was touching the handrail in an attempt to comfort the barge. It wasn't the words, the embarrassment, or even the practicalities of removing the paint and checking for damage: it was the attack on her boat. *Coralie* wasn't just her home and her business, but somehow a friend.

Were the blackmailers getting over-confident, since Fi would hardly let it go unreported, or emphasising that they meant business?

Passers-by slowed as they saw the graffiti. Some of the other liveaboards were approaching, plus a uniformed constable Fi didn't know.

'I don't get it,' said Dylan.

Fi took a deep breath. Her son wasn't a child. Looking at him now, with his arms folded and a scowl on his face, she could see what he would look like as a man, with elements of his father and Fi's brother. Stubbornness, trustworthiness, sensitivity. Hiding things from him wouldn't help. 'It's about the letter you had,' she murmured, putting her hand on his arm. 'After the police have finished, will you stay so that I can explain? And can you keep schtum about it?' She pointed at his mobile. 'Till we can talk?'

'S'pose so. What about customers?'

'I'm not opening today. I've already messaged Nerys and Zach.'

After the police officer had taken statements and prodded at the bank with no expectation of finding anything useful, one of the liveaboards offered to clean the paint off, as he'd been renovating another boat and had the equipment. She gratefully accepted the offer, helped him rope off an area to work in, then bought hot food from Willow's Wagon and went to join Dylan.

The pastries smelled fragrant and enticing, one filled with sausage and tomato, the other with curried chickpeas, but they remained untouched.

'Why isn't Marcus here?' said Dylan, pushing his mobile around the table.

'Graffiti isn't a detective thing.'

'But it's you. I'd have thought he'd be all over it like a rash. Maybe he doesn't care as much as you think. Or maybe he thinks it's true.'

'It isn't true and it's not that simple. That's what I want to talk about.'

Dylan sat back. 'Go on then.'

'I'm being blackmailed. Your letter and the graffiti is them increasing the pressure.'

Dylan's mouth dropped open. 'What have you done to be blackmailed about? Have you told Marcus? Or do you and Jade think you can solve it without him?'

Fi winced. 'We tried to outwit them on our own,' she said. 'That was my idea, and it didn't go too well.'

'Did they hurt you?' The scowl lifted enough for concern to shine through.

'They nearly hurt Jade, and it was my fault. After that, I told Marcus. He needs me to pretend I haven't told the police so they can catch them. That's why he didn't come about the graffiti. He wants me to send you to Annie's.'

'Get lost,' said Dylan. His scowl returned but he took a bite of the pastry. 'So, what *have* you done to be blackmailed about?'

'Nothing, but they're trying to implicate me in that woman's murder.'

Dylan's eyes widened. 'Why?'

'She visited me with a crazy story about your dad. I didn't want to tell you till I got to the bottom of it. Then she was murdered. But I don't think I can protect you without telling you. So here goes…'

After she'd finished explaining, Dylan blinked, then stood up and went to his cabin. She thought he'd grab his things and storm out. The tears which had been imminent all morning welled up, but didn't spill. She got up to make herself coffee, unsure what else to do.

'I'll do that,' said Dylan, appearing at her side. He gave her a one-armed hug that meant more than Fi could ever have expressed and ruffled her hair. 'Eat your pastry and look at this.' He handed over the notebook in which he jotted ideas for drama. 'See where the card's sticking out? Open it there. Don't get upset.'

Fi sat down again. She recognised the notebook: she'd found it at Christmas. She knew it contained photographs of Gavin and sketches of a father and son, and— She opened the book and gasped. Of course – how could she have forgotten? The Italian newspaper clipping with a photo of a man who looked like an older version of Gavin, which a former so-called friend had sent the previous October. She'd thrown it in the kindling basket for the log burner and Dylan must have fished it out.

Dylan thumped her coffee down and sat beside her. 'You're not the only one with secrets,' he said. 'I saw someone like that mooching round the river a while back. He's a bit like Dad and a bit not. Is he the bloke you saw?'

'Yes. That's why I haven't said anything.'

'I thought if he was Dad, he'd come and visit me . . . us. I didn't know what to think. I've been really miserable.'

Fi hugged him. 'I wish you'd told me. And your dad wasn't a horrible man. Just…'

'Weak?'

'He never thought of consequences. But he wasn't heartless. That's why I don't believe he's still alive.'

'Yeah?'

'Yeah.'

Dylan managed a wavering smile.

'I don't understand what the blackmailers mean

about me knowing something I haven't told anyone,' said Fi. She turned the page. Dylan had added prints of scanned photos. The originals must be from Annie's albums. 'Hold on. This one…'

'I thought it was nice.' Dylan shrugged. 'He looks relaxed and happy.'

'It's just like the one Bianca showed me of your dad from years ago, only from a different angle. I knew it was familiar, and now I remember. We were on a weekend break with a group of friends. I took this one, but someone else took the one Bianca had. It wasn't Italy at all. It was Cornwall. We were happy.'

She frowned as memories returned.

Seventeen years ago, Gavin had rented a big house with a view of the sea, to spend a few days with several couples who were friends of his. It was the sort of extravagant thing that he did and she thought they could afford, though she'd prefer they didn't.

Gavin had stayed up late into the night, but she hadn't. He'd slept in every morning, hungover, while she'd woken early and walked alone in the fresh sea air, feeling slightly nauseous even though she hadn't been drinking.

Why? Oh yes – she'd recently discovered she was pregnant and had only told Gavin. She didn't click with many of the women, and the men paid her no attention. They were too busy playing pool and darts and… There was that business plan to discuss, wasn't there? That was the whole point of the weekend.

Gavin had planned to go into real estate by creating a limited company, and wanted his friends to invest. A few did. Then, a year later, Gavin told her that it seemed too much like hard work and he'd sold the concept on. There had been no trace of it when she was sorting out the financial mess he'd left.

But what if someone thought the company had been transferred to her and she had a stash of money somewhere which she'd never declared? Someone who'd taken a photo of Gavin which they'd handed to Bianca as part of a plan to defraud her, and which Bianca in turn had showed to Simon so that he could help?

Dylan tapped the article. 'I tried an online translator, but the text's blurry. What came out made no sense.'

Fi cleared her throat. 'I know someone who may be able to help. She probably thinks I'm an idiot, but I can live with that. I just hope she's on duty in the right job.'

'What?'

'She volunteers as a special constable, but Marcus told me where she normally works. If she's volunteering, I'll have to think of something else. If she's at the building society I can pretend I'm getting cash, even though I don't have an account there.'

Dylan peeled the article off the page. 'Let's go. I've

got revision to do with Alfie. I'll stomp off like I hate you, and you get that translation.'

'So you don't hate me?'

'Not if you do chicken fajitas for tea.'

'All right, but don't stomp off on your own. Get your gang to fetch you.'

'I can take care of myself.'

'So can Jade. She still nearly ended up in the river.'

In the building society, two people sat behind a counter and a manager roamed about. Luckily, the manager was Liv.

'Can I talk to you in a booth concerning a withdrawal, please?' said Fi, glancing round to see if anyone was paying attention.

'Of course,' said Liv, a minuscule frown of recognition on her face. 'This way.'

'I don't really want money,' said Fi, as they sat down. 'It's something else.'

'Didn't we meet at the college yesterday? I didn't know you were a customer.'

'We did, and I'm not,' said Fi. 'But I'd appreciate it if you could pretend I am. Firstly, I must apologise for dragging you out of your lunch break yesterday to ask you odd questions. There was a good reason, and you were right to tell Marcus about the man you were talking to in the pub.'

'Marcus? Oh, Inspector Falconer.' Liv's eyebrows rose. 'You must be— Apology accepted. What's secondly?'

'This,' said Fi, passing over the newspaper cutting. 'Is the man in this photo the man you were comforting?'

'Not exactly comforting.' Liv held the cutting to the light. 'I'm pretty sure that's him, though.'

'Could he have been British but speaking Italian?'

'Anything's possible,' said Liv. 'But it's unlikely, as he was mostly talking in dialect. My family's from a different part of Italy, so I struggled to understand him. When people are distressed, they're more likely to revert to their native tongue. I'm ninety per cent certain that he was Italian born and bred and from Piedmont.'

'Can you translate the article?'

'I can try.' Liv smoothed out the paper. It had been screwed up in a ball, thrown into a dusty basket, flattened and glued to Dylan's book, then removed. It was a smudgy mess. 'It says that something blurred *"is proud of its Bocce team, which has beaten all local villages this year."*'

'Bocce?'

'It's an Italian version of boules.'

'Oh. What else does it say?'

'*"Marked out for special praise is Giorgio…"* Blur.' She pointed at the Gavinalike. '*"His wife says she'll be delighted to find a home for the trophy, and his team-mates say it must be in the blood. A worthy triumph!*'" She looked up at Fi. 'Does that mean anything?'

'It means everything,' said Fi. 'Can you get in touch with Marcus and tell him that? And can you give him this, too?' She handed over an envelope containing everything she could remember about Gavin's failed business enterprise. 'I think it'll make all the difference.'

CHAPTER 22

Jade stared at Netta. 'You need what?'

'Boxes,' said Netta. 'About this big.' She mimed a smallish cardboard box with her hands. 'I know exactly where to get them.'

'But what for?'

Netta managed to look pleased and apprehensive at the same time. 'Well, you said a small budget and limited stock, so...' She tapped on her phone and showed Jade the Crystal Dreams Facebook page. There was a new post at the top.

Not enough magic in your life? Now there can be! We're thinking of trialling a Crystal Dreams subscription box. Every month you'll get a box to make your day full of magic and good vibes. Check out the sample box in the pic! And remember – the first rule of Magic Club is that you tell EVERYONE about Magic Club! Who's in?

'I posted that yesterday at half four,' Netta said, proudly. 'Look how many likes and comments it's got.'

Jade clicked on the post and scrolled. 'Oh my.' She studied Netta. 'I assume you've costed it? Including postage?'

'Yup. Postage overseas is extra, of course, but in this country we'll be making around two pounds fifty per box. More if we have lots of subscribers, because we can buy in bulk.'

'We'll have to put the boxes together,' said Jade. 'While we're doing that, we aren't serving in the shop.'

'It's only once a month,' said Netta. 'We could get a Saturday girl. Or boy. And maybe we could offer a range of boxes, not just one. We could have themes—'

'Let's stick with one type for the trial, shall we?' said Jade. 'So where am I supposed to get these boxes? Not to mention the stock.'

'Does that mean I can put the order page live?' said Netta.

'We – we have an order page?'

'Yeah, it was easy. All I have to do is switch it on and put a link on our social media, and off we go.'

'Can I make tea first?' Jade went to the back room without waiting for a response and put the kettle on. *Well*, she thought. *Well*. As the kettle began to grumble, she got mugs from the cupboard.

Why didn't I think of subscription boxes? There's a subscription for everything these days.

Probably because you've been busy worrying about Fi. Give yourself a break, Jade, do.

Jade raised her eyebrows at her surprisingly sympathetic inner voice, then shrugged. *Maybe I will.* On that basis, she found an unopened packet of ginger nuts.

When she went into the shop, Netta's laptop was open on the counter. 'Shall I do it?' Netta asked, her finger hovering above the trackpad and a teasing smile on her face.

'What are you doing?' asked a young woman hovering by the card rack. She wore jeans and a black T-shirt with silver script which said *I can put a spell on you.*

'Oh, nothing much,' Netta said casually. 'Just launching a subscription box.'

'Subscription box?' The customer came over. 'What's in it?'

'It's different every month, but things like candles, incense, motivational cards, a piece of jewellery, maybe guidance on rituals and mantras, we could do stickers…'

'Oooh. How much is it?'

'Tenner a month.'

'That's a bargain. Go on, put it live.'

Jade put the mugs on the counter and Netta

watched her. 'Go on, Netta, you heard the woman.'

Netta bit her lip. 'I'm nervous.'

Jade grinned at her. 'People clearly want it. Go on, press the button.'

'OK…' Netta screwed her face up in a way that suggested she might be constipated and pressed the button, then heaved a great sigh. 'It's live. Do I share the link?'

'Of course you do!' said Jade, laughing. She watched Netta type and click, then picked up her mug and held it out. 'Here's to your new venture!'

Netta looked very serious. '*Our* new venture.' She picked up her mug, clinked Jade's, and took a sip. Then she glanced at the laptop and almost spat out her tea. 'Someone's signed up!'

The customer held up her phone. 'Do I get a prize for being the first?'

Jade considered. 'Tell you what, if you let us take a photo and put it in a social-media post about our new subscription box, I'll give you a £10 gift voucher.'

The customer beamed. 'Never hurts to ask, does it?'

Jade pulled out her phone. 'Netta, can you fetch our lovely customer a voucher and then get in the photo?'

Netta's eyes widened. 'Me?'

'Yes, you. You're subscriptions manager, so you should be in the photo.'

'I… Just let me brush my hair!' Netta grabbed her bag and scuttled to the bathroom.

Once the excitement was over and the customer had departed, Netta returned to the topic of the boxes. 'I looked online, but the best deal was from a company based in Monkton. If we buy a hundred or more, it's maybe two-thirds of the price of anything online.'

'Is that so,' said Jade. 'I assume one of us, namely me, would have to go and get them. As it happens, though, I fancy a trip to Monkton. I've got an invite to do a fete there, and it would be a good opportunity to check the place out. Maybe make some business contacts. You never know.'

'Sounds like a plan to me,' said Netta. 'And with' – she refreshed the screen on her laptop – 'twenty subscribers already, I guess you should get moving.'

'I guess I should. Why don't you pop out and get yourself lunch, Netta, and then I'll set off. I'll try not to be too long, but I don't want you stuck here with no food.' *Especially if I accidentally end up having a lunch stop in Monkton.*

'On it,' said Netta, and was heading out of the door thirty seconds later.

***

Well, Jade thought, looking around her, *this is nice.*

She had gone to the box company first, on the basis of business before pleasure, negotiated a small discount on the first hundred boxes, and discussed further bulk orders with the manager. 'We go through Hazeby quite a lot,' he said, 'so we might be able to drop off further orders.'

'That's very kind,' said Jade. 'But if I find a good spot for lunch, I'll be happy to pop over every so often.'

And walking down the high street, there were plenty. A Greek taverna, an Italian restaurant with gingham tablecloths and candles in chianti bottles, and any number of quaint pubs. *Excellent*, thought Jade, almost purring with satisfaction. *I'll do that fete, get extra help in, make sure I take breaks…*

A pub menu caught her eye and she moved closer, then gasped as someone cannoned into her.

'I'm terribly sorry – oh!' It was Simon from Spetisham Hall, flushing as if she had caught him stealing gobstoppers.

'Oh, hello there.' Jade smiled at him. 'Probably my fault. Wasn't looking where I was going.'

'I'm, um, here to sort out some advertising. For Spetisham Hall. As a wedding venue. People come from all over the county, not just locals.'

'I'm sure they do.' Jade kept a smile on her face, but behind it cogs were turning. *No business of mine why you're here, so why are you so keen to tell me?* 'How are you, Simon?' she asked. 'You seemed quite down when I last saw you. It was a terrible business.'

'It was,' he agreed. Strangely, he seemed less tense. 'I don't think they'll ever find out who did it. But it – it laid something to rest.'

'Oh yes?' Jade willed herself to keep her tone light. 'In what way?'

'Bianca was an old flame,' he said quickly, as if getting it all out would make it easier. 'When she came back to England, I wondered if we might— As it turns out, she was married. She kept it from me. Maybe she was embarrassed, or she thought I wouldn't help her if I knew, but... Anyway, water under the bridge now. Oh – no—' He went even redder.

'I know exactly what you mean,' said Jade.

'I – I'd better go. I have a meeting with a venue. Nice to see you, Jade.' And he hurried off.

Jade walked on a few steps, then ducked into a recessed doorway and peeped out. The street curved to the right, and she saw Simon stop at a pub, glance round, and dash in.

Hmm, she thought, and followed. She paused for a few seconds in the small, square entrance hall to get used to the darkness after the sunshine, then opened the door a fraction and peeked in.

The pub was doing good business. All the window tables were full. She let her gaze travel round the room, seeking Simon's pale-blue shirt. As she had suspected, he was at a table towards the rear. And he was with—

Her heart skipped a beat. *Double denim! And isn't that—*

The woman with him, who had been leaning over the table, suddenly sat back, looking cross.

The woman who tried to pump me about Fi! Jade hurried out and leaned against the wall, her heart pounding. *She said in the shop that they were going home the next day. So why are they still hanging around?*

She pulled out her phone, inched the door open, made sure her flash was off, and took a photo. Then she made for the car park. *Don't be silly*, she told herself. *They've got drinks to get through, and the only person who knows you're here is Simon, who had his back to you. You're safe.* Nevertheless, she broke into a trot.

When she reached Bertha, she got in, locked the doors and rang Fi. 'I'm in Monkton,' she said, as soon as Fi answered. 'Simon's here, being shifty, and he's having a drink with a couple I've met before. The woman came into the shop the Tuesday after the festival and she was trying to find out stuff about you. She talked a lot about money. She implied she wasn't local, but she's still hanging around nearby. And she thought you were doing very well for yourself.' She listened. 'Yeah, she's got blonde curly hair, chin length, and the man was wearing double denim. He

207

sort of followed her.' She gasped. 'So it's them?! Right, I'm coming straight back.'

Jade buckled her seatbelt, took a few deep breaths and turned the key. By a miracle, Bertha started first time.

Lunch would have to wait.

CHAPTER 23

After the graffiti incident, the other liveaboards visited with flowers, wine and chocolates for Fi and Dylan.

'If they do this to one of us, they do it to all of us,' said Angie, giving Fi a hug. 'We'll take it in turns to keep watch at night. Anything you need, give us a shout.'

'Thank you so much.' Fi felt rather overwhelmed by their support. 'I'm staying closed till Monday, but it's good to know you're here for us.'

Her relief that she and Dylan were less at risk faded the next morning when the postman delivered another letter.

Why don't you go and enjoy the music festival in the main square tomorrow? There's a bin in the corner, near a bollard. Drop the money in there at three, then leave. £20,000, like we said. We'll be tailing your son, so don't mess up. And don't tell the police or your spooky friend.

She contacted Marcus on the spare mobile he'd given her. He told her to go to the bank and speak to the 'new' manager, an undercover officer, who would give her marked money in a scruffy backpack with a tracker inside.

Afterwards, walking down the street carrying thousands of pounds, Fi felt as conspicuous as if she were naked and painted purple, with gold stars stuck on strategically. But no one paid her any attention whatsoever.

If she was being watched, why didn't the blackmailers mug her and take the money, rather than risk it being snatched before they got to it? Maybe the point wasn't just money, but something else too. Revenge? Humiliation? Gavin hadn't had that sort of nature. Besides, Fi was the one who theoretically deserved revenge, and she didn't have that sort of nature either.

She had just boarded *Coralie,* deep in thought, when Jade called from Monkton.

So Mel and Stefan were talking to Simon. Now Fi remembered that they'd been on that weekend break and Mel had been eager to invest in Gavin's idea. And it was Mel who'd sent her that Italian newspaper cutting, out of spite.

So that left the man who looked like Gavin. Where

was he? Maybe he'd been left behind to spy on her and Dylan, or maybe worse. But crying in the pub and talking to Liv suggested he might be a weak link. He must be staying around Hazeby somewhere, but Marcus hadn't tracked him down to any of the local hotels or self-catering places so far. Was he staying with friends, or someone in an Italian community that might exist in a bigger Wyvernshire town? If she and Jade could track *him* down, instead of the other way round, they might uncover the key to everything.

She sent a message to Jade: *I'll visit you at your flat in half an hour. I don't need to worry that anyone's following me, except that man, and I'd spot him within seconds.*

She put the bag of cash under a pile of jumpers at the bottom of her wardrobe, wishing she had burglar alarms set up all around the boat, then rang Alfie's house to confirm Dylan was there.

'Such a lovely lad,' said Alfie's mother. 'You must be so proud. Never a rude word or sulky expression. Not like my son: I can't do anything right.'

'Are you talking about the same Dylan?' said Fi. 'I never know whether Dylan will speak to me or ignore me these days, but Alfie's always delightful.'

'Really? That makes me feel better. And yes, they're revising. Though it seems to be music, not English Lit. Still, aren't they doing a mini gig at the music festival tomorrow?'

'Are they?'

'Apparently. The place will be heaving with musicians and dancers and you won't be able to move for tourists. Heaven knows how the police will keep order. Besides, they're still hunting that woman's murderer, aren't they? They won't be wasting time listening to bands and watching dance troupes.'

Hurrying out of the boat and locking up, Fi waved at Angie, who was waving from her narrowboat, and returned a thumbs up to another liveaboard on his cruiser. *Coralie* was as secure as she could be.

She paused for a second, wondering if she should stay, then told herself not to be a fool. *Again.* Turning abruptly, she walked straight into Leo Falconer.

At nearly eighteen, he was slightly taller and more broad-shouldered than his father, but otherwise he was a near carbon copy, though younger and less inclined to smile. At the moment, he didn't look as if he ever intended to smile again. His scowl was almost engraved on his face, his arms folded as if he expected an argument before he'd even said hello.

'Hi, Leo,' said Fi. She expected him to nod and stalk off to wherever he was going, but he continued to block her way.

'Can I ask you something?'

'Me? Er, yes, of course.' It was on the tip of her tongue to say that she didn't know where Marcus was, but it seemed unlikely that a teenage boy would actively seek his father. Then she remembered that Dylan had been talking to him recently. 'Is it about something you were discussing with Dylan?'

'In a way.' Leo hunched his shoulders. 'Parents are rubbish.'

Is that what Dylan says about me? Fi's face burned. 'What—'

'Mine are, anyway. Dylan says you give him more leeway.'

'Does he? Do I?'

'Yeah. Mum treats me like I'm four, and Dad, if he's not *busy*' – Leo sneered and made air quotes with his fingers – 'says the same old thing every time. Be responsible, get settled, put money in the bank. What does he say about me?'

'That he wishes he could spend more time with you, but the job—'

'That's why Mum and he split up when I was eight.' Leo relaxed a bit. 'He does try, though, I'll give him that. You're the only person he's been serious about since the divorce. He always put seeing me first, but now…'

Fi wondered if the conversation would go anywhere. She was desperate to get to Jade's, but didn't feel she could walk away while Leo was unburdening himself, even if she had no idea why he'd picked her as an audience. 'When children are becoming adults, they and their parents have to

213

redraw the boundaries. It's a bit painful for both, honestly. With your dad being in the police, he knows what can go wrong more than most. He knows the world isn't always a nice place.'

'His view's distorted!' Leo's scowl deepened. 'He needs to back off.'

'Do you want me to talk to him?' said Fi. 'Or is something wrong?' She felt anxious. Marcus had been worried about Leo's influence on Dylan and what he was doing in his spare time, fearing that his son wasn't concentrating on his studies and spending too much time with people Marcus didn't know. Did she really know what Dylan was doing with the group of teenagers she still thought of as kids?

'The world's an amazing place!' Leo almost shouted. 'I don't want to waste my life in a classroom when I could be exploring. I don't want to stare at lazy British rivers and green fields when I could be in deserts and mountains. I don't want to be stuck in pubs with stupid drunk students when I could be meeting interesting people from different cultures! When I know a bit more about the world, maybe I can help change the bad bits. But all Mum wants me to do is get a trainee manager's job in the supermarket so I can stay home. All Dad wants me to do is go to university then get some stinking office job sat in front of a computer – tap tap tap – till I'm as old as he is and I've missed the chance to live. I'd rather be like the guy in the woods – even he travelled to get here! I guess you don't understand either, but I thought…' Leo waved his hand at *Coralie* and gathered himself to storm off.

'I do understand,' said Fi, reaching for his arm. 'I did exactly what you say your dad wants you to do – university, office job, tapping at a keyboard until I thought I'd explode – but I had a dream and I worked for it. *Coralie* sort of saved me and Dylan. I don't know if your dad really wants you to do what you think he does – maybe it's come across wrong. I think your parents worry in case you fall in with a bad crowd. I'd be happy to ask your dad to—'

'Talk to me?'

'*Listen* to you.'

Leo puffed out a breath. 'All right. Look, I'm not in with any crowd – you can tell him that. I like being on my own. I've been wild camping to get away from them and get some life experience. I want to go off this summer and I won't let them stop me. I'm not doing A levels or going to uni.'

'OK,' said Fi. The last bit was Leo's parents' battle, not hers, but wild camping was different. She tried to sound casual. 'This person in the woods – is he another young man?'

'Young? Pfft. He's at least Dad's age.' Leo wrinkled his nose. 'He was all right to start with. His English isn't great but he showed me a few foraging and camping tricks. He's gone a bit weird, though. He cries at night in the shelter he's rigged up. It's the only reason I've gone home. Will you really make Dad listen?'

'I'll try. Thanks for trusting me, Leo.'

'Dylan said I could. I promised I'd let him know how the travelling goes, but before you panic, I'm not sure that's his scene. See you round.'

'See you, Leo. Take care.'

As he stalked off, Fi rushed towards Jade's, messaging Marcus from the spare mobile. She could have danced with joy when he answered that he was in town and could get to the flat before her.

A few minutes later, over a cup of tea, Fi described her meeting with Leo.

'Thanks for telling me what he's thinking,' said Marcus, with a brief smile. 'One less thing to worry about. In a way.'

'I promised you'd listen to him,' said Fi. 'Maybe you can compromise.'

'We must find the Gavinalike and sort out this murder and the blackmail first,' said Jade.

Fi waited for Marcus to correct 'we' to 'I', but he nodded. 'We do,' he said. 'And I've got good news of my own. I've been talking to the Italian authorities. They've looked through their records and reinvestigated the spot where Gavin's car went into the river. Something doesn't add up, Fi, but this time it's in your favour. Someone's gone missing from a small village in Piedmont, and they've found some remains which may be Gavin's.'

CHAPTER 29

Jade shifted from foot to foot and surreptitiously checked her watch. Five minutes to three. *Nearly time.* She winced as the saxophone player from a Madness tribute act which really ought to have been called Badness unleashed a raucous squawk. 'Let's get this over with,' she muttered.

In order to go undercover, she had crammed her hair under a baker-boy cap and put on a pair of jeans usually reserved for messy jobs around the house. As a result, she was sweltering. *At least Fi can wear normal clothes.*

And at least you aren't being blackmailed and framed for murder, she told herself.

She was about fifteen feet away from the bin where Fi was to put the money. It might as well have been a hundred, though, as the town square, a roughly triangular stretch of cobbles which had apparently once housed the town stocks, was heaving with people gripping plastic cups of beer and trying to hold conversations over loud ska music.

The band ground to a halt and the lead singer shouted 'Time for the grand finale – let's take "One Step Beyond"!'

Various middle-aged men shouldered their way to the front and started bopping, beer sloshing about them. Then Jade saw Fi's bright turquoise T-shirt moving towards the bin. It was all she could do not to watch. Perhaps half a minute later, she glanced round. There it was: a tatty old khaki backpack sitting on top.

'Excuse me,' said Jade, attempting to slide between two women comparing glitter tattoos. 'Just heading to the portaloo.'

'Bit too much information, love,' said one of them, and laughed.

A couple of minutes later, Jade had got herself to the back of the crowd. There she hovered, doing a knees-bend-and-swing dance and checking the bin every time she turned that way.

'One Step Beyond' seemed to go on for ever – certainly far beyond its welcome – but at last, with much use of cymbals, it drew to a close. The rucksack was still there. Jade bit her lip. The Wayfarers were supposed to play in half an hour, and Rick was watching one of the exits from the square. What if the blackmailers somehow managed to escape?

At least the money's marked and there's a tracker in the bag, she told herself. But her fists clenched at the idea of missing the chance to apprehend the people involved and tell them exactly what she thought of them.

The crowd was taking the opportunity of the changeover to catch up on their conversations. Jade listened, idly. Then someone yelled 'Conga!'

A ragged cheer rippled through the square.

A-ya-ta-da-da-daaaa-dah! A-ya-ta-da-da-daaaa-dah!

Onstage, the guitarist of the next band picked out the tune, grinning.

Where was it coming from? Jade peered into the crowd, but people were moving in front of her, craning to see, then running forward and joining the line. *A-ya-ta-da-da-daaaa-dah!*

Someone grabbed her round the waist from behind. 'I don't like congas!' cried Jade, wriggling.

'Neither do I, usually,' said Fi. 'I'm making an exception.'

Jade advanced on the bin, throwing in an occasional kick to the side. But the main conga line snaked across her path and all she could do was wait as various singing, swaying acquaintances, who really ought to have known better, wobbled past. When the bin finally came into view, the bag was gone.

Jade turned to Fi. 'We missed it!'

'We were meant to,' said Fi, grimly. She took out her phone. 'Time to unleash the tracker.' She opened an app and they watched a pulsing blue dot move down a side street. 'Let's go!'

Jade took the lead, on account of having sharp elbows and less concern for manners, and they hurried after it. Fi broke into a run and Jade did her best to keep up.

'It's no good,' Fi panted. 'They're getting away.'

'Hang on.' Jade pointed to a family sitting on a low wall, eating ice creams. A pink and a green scooter were propped next to them. She rushed over. 'Excuse me, could we borrow these?'

The woman narrowed her eyes. 'Aren't you...'

'Yes!' Jade pulled off her cap. 'And you're our first box subscriber!'

'Box?' said Fi.

'I'll explain later. We'll bring them back, honest.' Jade grabbed the pink scooter and whizzed off. 'Come on, Fi.'

'Turn right!' yelled Fi, in hot pursuit.

Jade obeyed. 'They would go uphill, wouldn't they,' she grumbled.

'Save your breath,' said Fi. 'I think I know where they're heading. The big car park.'

'Oh flip, that's miles away.'

They scooted along, weaving between knots of

people. Some cheered, while others scolded them for using wheeled transport on a road that was meant to be closed. 'You scooter people ought to be banned!' shouted a man in red trousers which almost matched his face.

'That explains how they got away so fast,' called Fi. 'E-scooter.'

Jade's phone rang. It was Rick's ringtone. She fished it out of her jeans pocket. 'Yeah?' she gasped.

'Where are you?'

'Chasing the money. Fi thinks they're going to the big car park.' A bump in the road made her fumble the phone and end the call.

'Not far now,' called Fi. 'Was that Rick?'

'Yeah.'

'Special ringtone?'

'Keep your eyes on the road.'

With great relief, Jade saw the sign for the car park. 'Take the next left!' yelled Fi. 'Shortcut!'

Jade's right foot ached from pushing and she felt as if the grinding rumble of the scooter's wheels would never leave her head. She turned left down a narrow alley which shook her bones, then emerged opposite the car park.

'The money's stopped moving,' murmured Fi. 'Back left corner.'

Suddenly, a smallish figure with short blonde curls ran across the car park and hammered on the window of a white car. 'Open the damn door!' she cried, then wrenched it open and dived in.

Jade and Fi exchanged glances. 'Now what?' said Fi.

'Not sure. I thought the police would catch up. If we stand in front of the car, they'll only run us over.'

'Well, that was definitely Mel,' said Fi, as the car's engine started. 'The tracker's still there. For now.' She sighed.

The car shot forward, swerved to avoid a parked car, and made for the exit. Jade's fists clenched again. But as the car reached the junction a police car blocked it, sirens blaring.

'Yes!' Jade punched the air.

The white car performed an alarming three-point turn and sped towards the other exit.

'Oh no!' cried Fi. 'The police will never turn round in time.'

'We'll get them,' said Jade, through gritted teeth. 'Eventually.'

The white car whined as it approached the other exit, but out of nowhere a van moved across the exit and stopped. A blue Transit with *The Wayfarers* stencilled on the side.

Brakes squealed as the white car skidded, spun round, then smashed to a halt against the car park information board.

Jade and Fi rushed to the car, which was hissing

and ticking. A man in double denim jumped out. 'Get out of there, Mel!' he cried, then muttered 'For heaven's sake,' opened the passenger door and hauled Mel out.

Marcus sprinted across the car park. 'Police! Everyone move away from the car.' Behind him was Sergeant Blake, moving at a more sedate pace.

'Glad to see you,' said Mel, lifting her chin. 'You're just in time to arrest a fraud and a murderer.'

'Really?' Sergeant Blake caught up to the group and took his notebook from his pocket.

'Yeah!' Mel pointed an accusing finger at Fi. 'She swindled us. She pretended her husband died so she could stash away a load of our money and she's been sitting on it ever since. When Bianca found her out, Fi killed her!'

'What?' Fi spread her palms. 'You've been trying to blackmail me! You've got a bag full of money in that car.'

'It was the only way to get back what's mine,' said Mel. 'You've got the police in your pocket, so I took justice into my own hands.'

Sergeant Blake pointed with his pencil. 'Here comes the cavalry, sir.'

They all turned. Rick was walking towards them, and with him—

'The Gavinalike!' murmured Jade, mesmerised.

Mel flung out an arm. 'See? That's him! That's her

husband. You're her husband, aren't you?'

The Gavinalike did not speak till he and Rick had reached the group. Then he cleared his throat. 'I am not this lady's husband.'

'Yes you are!' Mel scolded. 'Tell the truth – you're Gavin Booker! You've been hiding in Italy for years, and now you've come back to collect your money. Tell them!'

The Gavinalike turned to the police officers. 'I am not this Gavin, but I know of him. I was living in the next village when his car was found, years ago. It was very sad. I thought no more of it until this lady' – he indicated Mel – 'approached my wife and me and asked for our help. She told me it was a practical joke that would make money, and promised Bianca and me a share. I was unsure, but we were short of money and Bianca told me I must. If I had known…' He looked at his feet. 'If I had known what would happen…'

'You were a pawn in their game,' said Fi. 'I'm so sorry for your loss.'

The man burst into tears and Rick patted him awkwardly on the shoulder. 'I should have told the police!' he choked out. 'Bianca went to tell her she had changed her mind and we wouldn't be part of the joke any more. She never came back. I didn't know what to do. Bianca was gone, we had no money, and I couldn't get home… I tried to explain to the man Simon. We tricked him, used him. I was ashamed. But it was all their idea and it's all their fault.'

The man in double denim, who had seemed bewildered throughout this speech, turned to Mel. 'I don't get it. I said I wasn't sure this man was Gavin but you swore he was and the years in Italy had changed him.'

'It was the only way of getting what's owed to us, Stefan, you fool.'

Stefan turned to the police officers. 'It wasn't murder, it was an accident. We just meant to wave the boathook at Bianca, to scare her into carrying on, but Mel pushed her and the hook caught her dress as she fell—'

'I didn't push her, Stefan! I nudged her and she tripped!' said Mel. 'And we weren't scaring her. We were having a friendly chat—'

'With a boathook you'd stolen especially?' said Marcus. His phone buzzed and he checked it. 'Rick, would you mind moving your van? Our backup's here.'

Rick nodded and hurried away, but not before Jade had dashed over and given him a hug.

Marcus turned to Mel. 'Since you two have made a mess of your own car, we'll give you a lift in our nice roomy police vehicle.' Mel opened her mouth to speak and he held up a hand. 'I strongly suggest you don't make things worse for yourself.'

Rick's van started, then moved smoothly off. At

once, a police van pulled in and parked beside them. The passenger door opened and a sharp-suited woman with a blonde crop got out.

'Nina, good to see you,' said Marcus. 'Wondered if you'd mind giving me a hand with this bunch.'

Inspector Acaster's eyes gleamed. 'Nothing would give me greater pleasure,' she said. She glared at Mel and Stefan. 'Right, in the van with you. I'll do the speeches there.'

'I'll join you for that,' said Marcus. 'Sergeant Blake, would you mind taking this fellow to the station?' He indicated the Gavinalike, who held out his wrists.

'No call for that,' said Sergeant Blake, waving a hand. 'Come along now.' He shepherded the Gavinalike to the car, opened the back door for him, and turned to Fi and Jade. 'We'll need statements, of course, but well done.' He looked at the scooters, lying tangled together on the tarmac, and grinned. 'Maybe we should get police-issue ones.'

Jade giggled. 'I'd like to see Inspector Acaster chase a criminal on one of those.'

He chuckled. 'As would I.'

Jade put an arm round Fi as Sergeant Blake drove off. Fi sagged against her. 'I can't believe it's over.'

'Neither can I,' said Jade. 'I'm glad it is. With a little help from our friends.' She glanced at Fi, noting the purple shadows under her eyes. 'You look knackered. I can't decide whether you need a cup of tea, a stiff drink, or a good night's sleep.'

'I need all those things,' said Fi. 'But I'll settle for checking that Dylan and his band are safe, then a plastic cup of overpriced white wine and half an hour of folk music. Aren't Rick's band on soon?'

Jade checked her watch. 'In five minutes! Come on!' She bent and lifted the handle of the pink scooter. 'At least it's downhill this time.'

'I wouldn't say that,' said Fi, mounting the green scooter. 'I think things are looking up.'

CHAPTER 25

'So Hugo's visiting to help with the food and advise on the subscription service, huh?' said Fi, tilting her glass towards him. Hugo was listening intently to Netta as they stood at a barbecue, cooking for Jade's yard-warming party. There was a risk that the fancy artisan sausages he'd brought would be burnt if he didn't concentrate on them instead of the young woman beside him.

'Of course he is,' said Jade, offering a dish of assorted crisps that Hugo had bought at the delicatessen and mixed up for interest value. 'He *also* came to see if I'd followed all his design suggestions for the yard. Not that I did, but he seems to like what I've done.'

'Has he even noticed it?'

'He did when it was just the two of us.'

Fi contemplated her crisp. It appeared to have been

carved individually using a specialist chisel. 'What flavour's this supposed to be?'

'Posh goat cheese and thousand-year-old oak-aged balsamic vinegar, I think,' said Jade.

'What's a posh goat?'

'One too well-bred to make cheese that tastes of anything. Do you reckon Hugo will realise I've sneaked cheaper burgers in with the gourmet ones?'

Fi chuckled. Hugo's interest was focused on Netta, who was turning vegetable kebabs with one hand and waving the other at a shed which had been painted dark blue and decorated with silver stars. 'Did she decorate that shed or did you? The purple one has a different vibe. And I love the brackets for the overhead lights: they're really unusual. How did you get them up by yourself?'

Jade squirmed. In the weeks since the murder had been solved, she'd transformed the yard behind Crystal Dreams into a delightful space. She'd declared that the need for more storage had chivvied her into clearing the area, scrubbing away the moss and adding plants and two sheds, one to store boxes and one to sit in. It didn't seem remotely like the dank, dark area it had been a few weeks before. Now Jade had her own private outside space to enjoy, even if, filled with people and a barbecue on a summer evening, the word 'yard-warming' couldn't have been more apt.

Fi would have helped, but Jade had waved her offer away. 'You need a rest, Dylan needs your support during his GCSEs, and then you've got the Italy trip. I'll manage.'

Seeing it for the first time, two days after returning from Piedmont, Fi had wondered if Jade and Netta had really done it alone. Indeed, now that she thought about it, the sheds fitted the small space perfectly.

'All right, I admit it,' said Jade, at a hundred miles an hour. 'Rick made the sheds and seating and put the lights up. I couldn't have done it without him. He's a good *friend*.'

She stared at Fi as if daring her to argue, her whole frame tense, but Fi didn't rise to the bait. Jade's relationships were her own business. 'I'm glad. The more friends you have, the more settled you'll feel. Assuming you want to feel settled, that is.'

Jade relaxed a little and topped up their glasses, then looked across the yard at the friends she'd made since arriving in Hazeby, including Dylan and some of his pals. Chloe was one of the local girls hoping to get a Saturday job at Crystal Dreams, but that was up to Jade. Fi would probably pick someone less excitable. Netta must be bad enough.

Fi sat back and sipped her wine. Mellow music from a sound system created a pleasant backdrop.

She wondered what her friend was thinking. Did Jade want to settle? She was still renting. For that matter, Fi had had the chance to move away the previous year and hadn't taken it. But she lived on a boat, which by its very nature hinted at the possibility of going somewhere else. She recalled the books Dylan had taken from the shelves after talking to Leo: global cycling and camping off the beaten track. Leo hadn't thought Dylan would want to do it, but did he? And how would she feel if he did?

'I'm sorry you didn't get to see Italy for the first time in happier circumstances,' said Jade, shaking her out of her thoughts. 'And I'm sorry I haven't given you the chance to debrief. I understand if you don't want to talk about it.'

'It's OK,' said Fi. 'It was hardest for Annie and Nigel, really. But even for them, there was a kind of relief. The remains they found were under rocks downriver, and might never have been found if Marcus's investigation hadn't made the police check again. There weren't many, but – without being too graphic – they could get DNA to prove they were Gavin's and that he's been dead all this time. Poor thing.'

'Annie, or Gavin?'

Fi looked into her wine. A brief image of Gavin as he'd been when they were happy drifted into her mind, then dissolved. 'Both.' She heaved a sigh and gave Jade a half-smile. 'Clichéd as it is, we have closure now – including Dylan. And Gavin's family has a real grave to visit. Italy was breathtakingly beautiful and everyone was so kind. One day, Dylan and I will go back. I'd even go to Piedmont again – just not that village and that river. I suppose Dylan might.'

'He might,' said Jade. 'Or he might not. Deal with it when it happens.' She gave Fi a quick hug, then clinked glasses with her. 'To new beginnings.'

'To new beginnings, and exams being over.'

Jade shuddered. 'Even the thought of exams makes me feel faint,' she said. 'I'm looking forward to that jamming session on *Coralie*'s deck.'

'We're not allowed within fifty metres.'

'Huh,' said Jade. 'I don't believe you'll let a bunch of teenagers loose on your boat without being close enough to push them in the river if necessary. You're too much of a control freak. Here, have an aristocratic chicken and antique herb crisp. That'll strengthen you.'

Rick sauntered over and sat down. 'I hope you don't mind, Fi, but I've been talking to Dylan. The Wayfarers are doing a mini-tour over the summer. Towns and villages in Wyvernshire – no overnights, just little festivals. Anyway, he asked if he could come along and help with staging and general roadie stuff. I'd be happy if you are. He'd be paid, of course. I promise he'd be all right.'

Fi looked beyond him to Dylan, who appeared not

to be watching even though she knew he was. She felt slightly scared, but also excited.

'I may be at one or two of the gigs,' said Jade airily. '*If* I am, I can keep an eye on Dylan.'

'Sounds good,' said Fi. 'Come round tomorrow evening and have a chat with both of us, Rick.'

Rick grinned. 'Cool. Now, I'm going to find suitable music to listen to while eating charred chicken kebabs.'

'He hasn't burnt them, has he?' said Jade, glaring at Hugo, who was frantically scraping at something. 'I marinated those myself. It's my special recipe. The only thing he'd let me do.'

'It'll be fine,' said Fi. 'Stop worrying.'

'Says the woman who's having veggie burgers. What can go wrong with those?'

'The fact they're not cooked because he's forgotten to put them on the barbecue?'

'Oh, flip.' Jade rolled her eyes and rose to her feet. Then she paused. 'Fi, is Marcus sick of us interfering in his investigations? Or is a yard not posh enough for an inspector, even with fancy crisps? I mean, he is coming, isn't he? He's . . . you're . . . he's not...'

'How many questions is that?' said Fi, picking out a crisp which might or might not be heritage tomato and ancestral garlic. 'What are you, the Spanish Inquisition?'

'Seriously.'

'Number one,' said Fi, counting on her fingers, 'he needed our help with the investigation. He'll never say so, but it's true. Number two: your yard is now far too fancy for the police and he should be glad you invited him. Also, he can use his investigating skills to work out what the fancy crisps are supposed to be, then get food from the minimart if he wants. And finally, here he is, coming through the gate. He's been taking Leo to the airport. He looks like he needs a drink, but he's stopped to talk to Hugo because of all the smoke.'

Jade turned. 'Aargh! It's not even as if I like cooking, people or parties. Why did I get talked into this?'

'I thought it was your idea.'

'Yeah, well…' Jade stomped towards her son, grabbing a beer from a cooler and handing it to Marcus on her way to the barbecue.

Marcus came over, pausing to greet people, and dropped into the chair Jade had vacated. He seemed tired and subdued.

Fi put her hand on his. 'How did it go?'

'He's promised to return at the end of summer to finish school and take his A levels.'

'Don't you believe him?'

'The job with the bicycle tour company ends in August, but the tours go on till October…'

'He'll be back.'

Marcus sighed. 'The company said they couldn't

take him on in September if he hadn't finished his education. But he'll be a caged animal during his final year at school.' He ran his hand over his face. 'When his mum wasn't listening, I told Leo that I understood and I wished it was different for him, like it was for us. I started with the police at his age and worked my way up. I never did A levels. No one made me stay in a classroom.' He grinned. 'Apart from a police one.'

'He will come back.'

'Yeah, I think he will. It's just one year, and he can see that it'll open up more options if he can stick it out. His mum's devastated. She's seen the writing on the wall: in a year's time, he won't be in a nice safe job at home or at university, but heading out to trek the world. She'll miss him so much – so will I – but at the same time...' Marcus entwined his fingers with Fi's.

'You're kind of excited for him and kind of jealous of him?'

Marcus looked up. 'How did you know?'

'Because I understand,' said Fi. 'Because I love you.'

His face filled with joy and he cupped her cheek. 'I love you too,' he said. 'One day soon, shall we have our own adventure? One that doesn't involve murder but a nice break a long way away, with food, and wine, and...'

'That sounds like a plan,' said Fi, and kissed him.

WHAT TO READ NEXT

If you've enjoyed reading Fi and Jade's fourth case together, watch out for the next book in the series: *Murder at Work*.

Halloween is approaching, and Jade is looking forward to bumper profits for Crystal Dreams – until another magic shop opens its doors. And the shop manager isn't above stealing their ideas…

Jade's furious, and sparks fly between her and her assistant Netta as they fight over the best way to keep Crystal Dreams afloat. But that pales into insignificance when the rival shop manager is found dead – and all the evidence points to Jade.

That isn't Jade's only problem. She's been running away for years – but a chance photograph leads someone from her past straight to her.

Check out *Murder at Work* at https://mybook.to/ MurderAtWork.

If you've enjoyed reading a co-written book, Caster and Fleet Mysteries is a six-book series we wrote together, set in 1890s London. Meet Katherine and Connie, two young women who become friends in the course of solving a mystery together. Their unlikely partnership takes them to the music hall, masked balls, and beyond. Expect humour, a touch of romance, and above all, shenanigans!

The first book in the series is *The Case of the Black Tulips,* and you can read all about it here: http:// mybook.to/Tulips.

If you love modern cozy mysteries set in rural England, *Pippa Parker Mysteries* is another six-book series set in and around the village of Much Gadding.

In the first book, *Murder at the Playgroup*, Pippa is a reluctant newcomer to the village. When she meets the locals, she's even more reluctant. There's just one problem; she's eight months pregnant.

The village is turned upside down when a pillar of the community is found dead at Gadding Goslings playgroup. No one could have murdered her except the people who were there. Everyone's a suspect, including Pippa...

With a baby due any minute, and hampered by her toddler son, can Pippa unmask the murderer?

Find *Murder at the Playgroup* here: http:// mybook.to/playgroup.

Finally, if you love books and magic, welcome to the *Magical Bookshop*! This six-book series combines mystery, magic, cats and of course books, and is set in modern London.

When Jemma James takes a job at Burns Books, the second-worst secondhand bookshop in London, she finds her ambition to turn it around thwarted at every step. Raphael, the owner, is more interested in his newspaper than sales. Folio the bookshop cat has it in for Jemma, and the shop itself appears to have a mind of its own. Or is it more than that?

The first in the series, *Every Trick in the Book*, is here: http://mybook.to/bookshop1

ACKNOWLEDGEMENTS

First, as always, thank you to our marvellous beta readers – Carol Bissett, Ruth Cunliffe, Christine Downes, Stephen Lenhardt, Carmen Radtke and Julia Smith – and to our eagle-eyed proofreader, John Croall. Thank you for your assistance! Any errors that remain are our responsibility.

And many thanks to you, dear reader! We hope you've enjoyed the latest instalment in Fi and Jade's adventures. If you have, please consider leaving a short review or a rating on Amazon and/or Goodreads. Reviews and ratings are very important to authors, as they help books to find new readers.

COVER CREDITS

Image: Depositphotos.
Cover fonts:

Fairing by Design and Co.

Dancing Script OT by Impallari Type: https://www.fontsquirrel.com/fonts/dancing-script-ot. License: SIL Open Font License v1.10: http://scripts.sil.org/OFL.

ABOUT LIZ HEDGECOCK

Liz Hedgecock grew up in London, England, did an English degree, and then took forever to start writing. After several years working in the National Health Service, some short stories crept into the world. A few even won prizes. Then the stories started to grow longer…

Now Liz travels between the nineteenth and twenty-first centuries, murdering people. To be fair, she does usually clean up after herself.

Liz's reimaginings of Sherlock Holmes, her Pippa Parker cozy mystery series, the Caster & Fleet Victorian mystery series (with Paula Harmon), the Magical Bookshop series, and the Maisie Frobisher Mysteries are available in ebook and paperback.

Liz lives in Cheshire with her husband and two sons, and when she's not writing or child-wrangling you can usually find her reading, messing about on

Twitter, or cooing over stuff in museums and art galleries. That's her story, anyway, and she's sticking to it.

Website/blog: http://lizhedgecock.wordpress.com
Facebook: http://www.facebook.com/
lizhedgecockwrites
Twitter: http://twitter.com/lizhedgecock
Goodreads: https://www.goodreads.com/lizhedgecock

ABOUT PAULA HARMON

Paula Harmon is a civil servant, living in Dorset, married with two adult children. Paula has several writing projects underway and wonders where the housework fairies are, because the house is a mess and she can't think why.

For book news, offers and even the occasional recipe, please sign up to my newsletter via my website.

https://paulaharmon.com
viewauthor.at/PHAuthorpage
https://www.facebook.com/pg/paulaharmonwrites
https://www.goodreads.com/paula_harmon
https://twitter.com/Paula_S_Harmon

BOOKS BY LIZ HEDGECOCK

To check out any of my books, please visit my Amazon author page at http://author.to/LizH. If you follow me there, you'll be notified whenever I release a new book.

The Magical Bookshop (6 novels)
An eccentric owner, a hostile cat, and a bookshop with a mind of its own. Can Jemma turn around the second-worst secondhand bookshop in London? And can she learn its secrets?

Pippa Parker Mysteries (6 novels)
Meet Pippa Parker: mum, amateur sleuth, and resident of a quaint English village called Much Gadding. And then the murders began…

Booker & Fitch Mysteries (4 novels, with Paula Harmon)
Jade Fitch hopes for a fresh start when she opens a new-age shop in a picturesque market town. Meanwhile, Fi Booker runs a floating bookshop as well as dealing with her teenage son. And as soon as they meet, it's murder…

Caster & Fleet Mysteries (6 novels, with Paula Harmon)

There's a new detective duo in Victorian London . . . and they're women! Meet Katherine and Connie, two young women who become partners in crime. Solving it, that is!

Mrs Hudson & Sherlock Holmes (3 novels)

Mrs Hudson is Sherlock Holmes's elderly landlady. Or is she? Find out her real story here.

Maisie Frobisher Mysteries (4 novels)

When Maisie Frobisher, a bored young Victorian socialite, goes travelling in search of adventure, she finds more than she could ever have dreamt of. Mystery, intrigue and a touch of romance.

The Spirit of the Law (2 novellas)

Meet a detective duo – a century apart! A modern-day police constable and a hundred-year-old ghost team up to solve the coldest of cases.

Sherlock & Jack (3 novellas)

Jack has been ducking and diving all her life. But when she meets the great detective Sherlock Holmes they form an unlikely partnership. And Jack discovers that she is more important than she ever realised…

Halloween Sherlock (3 novelettes)
Short dark tales of Sherlock Holmes and Dr Watson,
perfect for a grim winter's night.

For children
A Christmas Carrot (with Zoe Harmon)
Perkins the Halloween Cat (with Lucy Shaw)
Rich Girl, Poor Girl (for 9-12 year olds)

BOOKS BY PAULA HARMON

THE MURDER BRITANNICA SERIES
Murder Mysteries set in 2nd Century Britain
mybook.to/MurderBritanniaSeries

THE MARGARET DEMERAY SERIES
Historical Mysteries set in the lead-up to World War 1
mybook.to/MargaretDemeraySeries

OTHER BOOKS BY PAULA HARMON
https://paulaharmon.com/books-by-paula-harmon/

**SHORT STORIES BY PAULA HARMON & VAL
PORTELLI**
viewbook.at/PHWeirdandpeculiartales

AUDIOBOOKS BY PAULA HARMON
https://paulaharmon.com/audiobooks/

WHITE
RHINO
BOOKS

Printed in Dunstable, United Kingdom